M.J. KELLY

D1715122

Brad's
Revenge

Judith,

~~Hope~~ Hope you enjoy the read!

Mitzi J. Kelly.

Outskirts Press, Inc.
Denver, Colorado

Brad's Revenge
All Rights Reserved

Outskirts Press
http://www.outskirtspress.com

ISBN-10: 1-59800-647-9
ISBN-13: 978-1-59800-647-6

Outskirts Press and the "OP" logo are trademarks belonging to Outskirts Press, Inc.

Printed in the United States of America

In Memory Of

Real old cowboys and friends'
Jack
Shorty and Pard

Special thanks to my husband and best friend Chet

CHAPTER 1

When Brad rode up, the first thing he saw was the reason for the gate being open and lying down on its side. Now as anybody who lives in cattle country knows, gates were meant for one of two things, to keep stock in or to keep something out. Looking down at the rusty broken hinge, a dark curious look came across his unshaven face. Slowly his eyes moved to scan the fence that ran up along the road. It was plain to see that no one had ridden fence or made repairs for quite sometime. The wire was lying down on the ground and in some places' weeds had grown up and around the sagging posts. With a silent signal he started his horse and advanced further up the road, his eyes viewing the disrepair and neglect as he went. The only sound created was from his large chested dun colored horse as he walked along the road, stirring up puffs of dust with each stride that he took. Brad could feel the silence around him so strong that he had to shake himself to get rid of the desolate feelings that were consuming him. He knew it wasn't far to the homestead and he was thinking how good it was going to feel to be back after all this time. When he came into sight of the outside corral, he pulled up short. It was completely empty and had been for a long time from the looks of all the tall dry grass and weeds that had grown. It was completely devoid of any stock that it ordinarily held. Spinning his horse around with a light touch, he headed for the water trough. Stopping he looked down and could see that it was dry and full of dirt as if it had never held water in the past. Sliding off his saddle with a grace only someone with years of living on the trail can accomplish, Brad stood and took in the sights around him. It was to quiet. Except for a few birds fluttering around, there was no sign of life or movement anywhere. His glance moved over to the left, landing on the sight where the bunkhouse stood across from the corral. The whitewash building with its slopping porch across the front that he remembered so well was totally destroyed. Now standing there was only a pile of old burnt rubble. Scanning further over he could see that the large barn that had stood down at the end of the road hadn't fared any better. All that remained was a skeleton of blackened charcoal timbers and the hitching rail standing abandoned and desolate.

Brad took a deep breath and turned slightly. He

looked up toward the knoll where he knew the house stood and closed his eyes at the sight. The house and all that he remembered were no longer there. Walking up to the area that once had been a full blooming flower garden, he found the only things growing there now were stalks of brown dried weeds, the flowers having long since dried up and disappeared. His gaze lifted up to what should have been a white house complete with a wide verandah sitting on a sloping yard with green grass shaded by a big beautiful oak tree, instead there was only a shell of a building that had once been a home. The roof had collapsed into the bottom floor and large desolate black beams stuck up into the air as if they were pointing to the sky. Perched on one side of the rubble, a charred brick chimney still stood tall as if to remind anyone passing that this place had once been a warm inviting asylum. In shock at all of the destruction he is seeing, his mind is running wild. Where is everybody? Who or what could have done this and why?

Brad walked over to where his big dun was standing with the reins on the ground. He took off his gear and loosened the saddle cinch. Walking over to the water trough, he started pumping the handle with a shaking fierceness that was flowing through his whole body. When the cool brownish water came out, he stuck his head under the spout, letting the water run down and over the dirt and dust accumulated during his long hot ride.

It felt cold, but it cleared his head and refreshed his mind from the numb state it was in. A snort behind him and a nudge came, as his stocky dun had smelled the water and put his nose in the trough for a drink. Brad kept pumping the handle until there was enough water to clear the mud off the bottom and fill it. Dun put his mussel deep inside the trough and stirred the water around before settling down and taking deep gulps of the cold water.

"Well Dun, this isn't exactly the homecoming I had been thinking of, can't for the life of me figure this out." Dun lifted his head out of the trough and twitching his ears forward looked over at Brad. He was used to hearing Brad talk to him. They should have a strong bond between them after spending so many years together on the trail. With a pat on Big Duns neck, Brad turned and took his canteen off the saddle.

Filling his canteen full of cold water and grabbing some hard tack out of his gear, Brad walked up the knoll to a large oak tree that had been the main source of shade in the yard for years. When he looked up into its large wide branches, he saw that the rope swing was still hanging down from them, just as it did years back. Sitting down he took off his hat and laid it down beside him. Drawing up his knees he put his elbows on them and cradled his head in his hands. After a while he raised his arms and ran his fingers through his thick dark hair, then stretched out his six foot hard lean frame, browned and toned to perfection from all the years working on the cattle trails. The laugh lines in the corners of his clear blue eyes betraying the cold feelings that were inside him as he looked out over what had once been his home.

Rising, Brad walked over to what remained of the house. Scouting the perimeter of the building, it didn't take him long to find where the fire had started. It was easy to see that someone had deliberately set it. What he could not find was the answer, why this could happen, and by who.

Brad worked his way into the pile of rubble, pushing burnt beams out of his way as he went. The smell of ashes hitting his senses each time he took a step and stirred up the dust. In a few short moments he stopped and with a deep frown crossing his features he looked around slowly. Thinking that if he guessed right he should be in the area of the study. Lifting a few more beams out of his way, he found what he was looking for. The safe was lying on its back, and it only took one glance to see that the door was intact and closed. Bending over he turned the dial and found that it still worked. It wasn't long before Brad had it open and was looking inside. "Now what the heck," Brad mumbled to himself as he stared down into an empty safe. "Who would empty a safe and then lock the darn thing back up again? Especially if you're going to burn the place down." There were only three other people that knew the combination to that safe beside himself and he knew they weren't the ones responsible for this, so who could have done it? Looking once again into the safe, Brad noticed something lying down in the far corner. Reaching in he picked up the object. Turning it over in his hand he recognized it as his fathers watch. It was untouched by the fire having been in the safe at the time. Gripping it firmly in his fist, Brad turned and headed out of the ruins into the fresh air. He stopped and took a few deep breaths before he continued on down the slope toward his horse big Dun.

Walking up to his gear Brad let out with a short whistle. He didn't have to turn around to know Dun was walking up to him, he could hear the thud of his hoofs as they hit the dry brown dust.

It wasn't long before Brad was traveling down the same road he had ridden up on earlier that morning, only his mood was a lot darker now then it had been. Giving Dun a pat he said, "let's move boy it seems like we have our work cut out for us."

CHAPTER 2

C hase stood at the end of the long worn bar with a glass in his hand. Hot, dusty and tired, he was thinking of how good it felt that the long drive was finally over. After Brad gets back from settling things at the ranch, all they have left to do is drive the herd a short distance and six years of hard work will finally come to an end. Reaching into his denim shirt pocket beneath his vest, he pulled out the makings for a smoke. Taking his time he poured tobacco on the paper and rolled it to a perfect fit. His hand reaching up to his flat brim hat, he found the wooden match that he was looking for in his rattlesnake hatband. While lighting up his glance took in the surroundings around him. The room was long and narrow with a high ceiling, the bar running the full length of it on one side, the back bar was an ornate carved piece that stood from floor to ceiling with gas lamps mounted about every four feet. On the other side of the room were tables along the wall. The chairs were setting upside down on the tables to allow the old gent who was sweeping, access underneath them without any obstacle. Besides the old man cleaning up and the bartender, Chase was the only other person in the room. Still it was early in the morning and most of the crowd wouldn't be coming in until around noon when the food was set out. As most of the saloons do at that time of the day, they would put out the normal fanfare of sliced beef or pork, large soft pretzels and crackers with cheese. All well salted to assure that plenty of liquid was bought to wash it down. Chase took a swallow of his drink and yelled. "Hey barkeep, I'm going to need you to setup a round of drinks for my boys when they get here." "They're all going to be mighty dry, after the miles they put on."

The bartender, a beady red eyed, nervous little man with brown thinning hair and a large porous nose turned and looked down at the end of the bar. He had noticed the stranger when he first came in, not because he was so big, actually he was of average height and weight dressed in the normal cowhands working garb. His brownish hair was a little longer then the townsfolk wore it, hanging well down over his collar, but other then that it was more the feeling of strength the man showed in the way he walked and the atmosphere of power that he generated. The way he wore his gun on his left hip, strapped to his leg with an ease that it was there since he was born, would tell anyone that he was a man able to take matters into his own hands. When he had served him his first drink, the stranger smiled and had a friendly manner about him, but that did not take away the look that seemed to go right through you.

"And where might they be coming from?" the barkeep asked.

"Down south, close to Mexico, me and my partner Brad bought up a nice size herd to bring up to his ranch near here."

The bartender looked long and thoughtful at the man who was standing in front of him. He could tell this stranger was not a man to rub the wrong way.

"This Brad fella you're talking about, you say he's from around here and has a ranch somewhere close?"

"That's right barkeep, he left early this morning to head out there to set everything up for us to take the herd out in the morning."

"Well. The only Brad I can remember around here is from the old Steven's spread, but he's been gone for years and nobody has heard a word from him since he left."

"Yep, that's Brad all right, he never was one for writing."

"Now if it's the same Brad I'm thinking on, the barkeep said. He ain't going to find much of a ranch when he gets out there."

Chases' hazel eyes turned hard on the skinny man and the friendly smile had left his face, the change was so fast that the bartender wasn't even sure he had seen it happen.

"What are you talking about?" asked Chase in a

soft low voice.

"Well all the Steven's are gone and the place is deserted. There hasn't been anyone living out there for about three years now."

"Gone? What do you mean gone, gone where?"

The bartender was getting nervous. He should have kept his mouth shut. He could see the anger in this stranger and he didn't want to be the one to tell him anything that might set him off.

"I'm not sure, he said. Maybe you need to go over and talk with the sheriff, he may be able to tell you something."

Chase slammed down his glass and started to turn toward the door when he saw Brad coming in with a look on his face that would tell anyone who knew him not to get in his way.

Brad stopped just inside the door, spotting Chase he started toward him. Chase seeing Brad coming into the bar, swallowed the last of his drink and set down his glass. He then turned and started toward Brad. Meeting halfway across the room Brad stopped. Chase looking at his best friend knew, without asking, that something was deadly wrong.

"Chase, where's the boys?"

"Why they should just be finishing up getting the herd down at the camp. They were going to come into town later on."

"Well, you ride on out and tell Ornery to get all the boys to herd the cattle on out to the ranch. Tell him to set up camp at the lower pond. He knows the way and after that meet me back in town, I'll probably be over at the Sheriffs' office."

"Sure thing Brad, *I'm* on my way." Chase knew better then to question him when he was like this. Brad would tell him in his own sweet time when he was ready. He had an inkling though; that it had something to do with what the bartender had told him about the Steven's place being deserted.

The bartender was watching the exchange between Brad and Chase. When he saw them finally walk out through the swinging doors, he breathed a sigh of relief. He's not for sure what happened out there at that Brad fellow's ranch, but one thing he knew for sure was that if anyone did have something to do with that fire out there, he wouldn't want to be around when them two fellows found them.

Shuffling around to the other side of the bar, he proceeded to walk over to the window. Looking out he watched as the fellow he had been serving drinks to, mounted on his horse and headed out of town. The other fellow was starting to walk down towards the sheriffs office.

Chase mounting up on his peg pony Slide, was deep in thought as he headed out of town towards camp. He knew Ornery could take care of things as far as the heard went and he knew his way around the country. They had good hired hands, in fact Chase would put them up against any working man out there. One thing he didn't know was what happened out there at Brad's ranch, and where is everyone that was there.

CHAPTER 3

"**N**ow doggone it Pard don't be bugging me right now. Can't you see I'm busy trying to get this gear packed and ready to go, so we can move out in the morning when Brad gets here?" Pard, was a mix of every kind of dog imaginable. He was the size of a full-grown goat, with long shaggy hair and a loyal disposition beyond compare. Pard just stood there with his head cocked to one side, listening to the one and only thing in his life that he can ever remember. Looking at Ornery Jack's short stubby legs and pot belly, Pard's tail started making signs in the dirt as he wagged it back and forth. Ornery Jack stood up and felt the stiffness in his back and legs. "Gettin old Pard, bones just don't seemed oiled anymore like they used to." Ornery's hand came up and pushed his long gray hair out of his face, then picking up his old mud caked hat he put it on. Reaching down he gave Pard a rough playful pat on his head; they've been together ever since Ornery found him as a half-drowned pup on the trail years back. You never saw one without the other. Most of the time on cattle drives, dogs weren't too popular because of the havoc they caused, but Pard was an exception because he's pulled his worth on more than one occasion.

"Anyway Pard." Ornery Jack said as he started to finish loading, "after tomorrow were going to be back home again. Wait until you meet little Kate! She'll keep you on your toes. She's the cutest tomboy you ever could meet." Ornery stopped and pulled a plug out of his back pocket, bit off a chunk and stuck it in his lip.

Pulling out his old bandanna he wiped the spittle off his long graybeard and mustache. Replacing his kerchief into his pocket, Ornery looked at Pard and said, "Now where was I? Oh yea, that missy can ride a horse near as good as any man I ever seen and her only being ten years old, well no telling what she can do now with me being gone all these years." Ornery stopped and turned his head, then he let loose with a stream of tobacco juice towards a lizard that was sitting on a rock sunning himself. "Got him Pard, dead in the head." Pard was use to Ornery's wild yelling when he let loose with that tobacco. He always hit what he shot at.

Suddenly Pard jumped up and started barking. Ornery scanned the area that Pard was looking at when he spotted a rider coming into camp a hell bent for leather.

When the oncoming rider got close enough, Ornery saw it was Chase. "Now what in the sam hill has gotten into him?" he said half to himself and half to Pard.

When Chase saw the camp, he swung his peg pony toward Ornery Jack's wagon. As he pulled up, his short-legged roan tucked in and slides to a stop, just as he was swinging down off the saddle.

"Ornery we got trouble," Chase said as he walked up to where Ornery was standing.

"Why Chase? What's up?"

"I'm not really sure.," said Chase. *Thinking that he should keep what he had heard from the bartender to himself until he got back to town and found out for sure what was going on.* "Brad came back to town madder then a throw back horse. He told me to tell you to get the herd started out to the ranch and to set up camp down at the lower pond. He said you'd know were. I'm going back to town to meet with him."

Walking back to his roan, Chase stepped up into his saddle, and turning to Ornery Jack he said, "most likely we'll meet up with you at the ranch later on." Then spinning his roan around he put him in a full run back toward town.

Ornery stood there a moment watching Chase ride off wondering what could have happened to get Brad so all fired up.

"Well Pard we better do as were expected." At that Ornery looked over to where his four mules were staked out. He let out a sigh, knowing what he was going to go through. He went to the wagon and got his rope. Those four half broken mules were mean to hitch up, and bridle shy as well, but they would take that wagon anywhere he asked When his cook wagon had to get somewhere in a hurry to get camp setup, that could mean taking all kinds of short cuts between boulders, up the side of a mountain or across raging creeks and steep sided streams. No matter, they always come through when Ornery called on them for their best.

After he had them all hooked up and the gear tied down, he climbed up on the wooden seat and released the break. He picked up his long black-snake bullwhip and with a flick of his wrist he sent the tail of it up, over and out with the perseverance of years as an old time mule skinner, yelling and cussing at them the whole time. Finally the mules started pulling on their shackled traces.

Ornery drove his wagon over to where the herd was just settling down for the day. Looking around the area he spotted Shorty walking towards the rumada.

"Shorty" Ornery called out.

Hearing his name, Shorty turned to see where the yell had come from. Standing about five feet six inches in his stocking feet and sporting a long handled bar mustache and a beat up old hat with the brim pinned up in front, he didn't give the impression of being one of the best horse wranglers in the country. Having lived in the South West all his life he had learned riding and roping from the vaquero's who were the best to be found and Shorty had learned well.

There weren't many things that he couldn't snare in his rope when he threw it. He very seldom missed and there wasn't a horse alive that he was afraid to get on and ride. Anyone who was lucky enough to get a horse that Shorty broke, knew he wouldn't have to buck them out in the morning and that horse would cut a cow out or die trying.

Walking over towards Ornery, his chaps dragging over the top of his boots as he went, Shorty came up to the wagon with a questionable look on his face.

"What are you doing here this time of day Ornery?"

"Looks like we got some trouble Shorty. Don't rightly know what it is just yet. All I know is Chase came out and said that Brad wants us to get the herd moved on out to the ranch. Since Brad and Chase aren't here it looks like you will have to fill in as trail boss till we reach the ranch. You can get Curly to take over as wrangler for the time being. You go on out and instruct the boy's to start moving the herd, I'll take the point so you can all follow."

"Sure thing Ornery, I'm on my way."

Shorty turned and headed toward his horse, hearing Ornery yelling and cussing at his mules as he cracked his whip to get them moving.

While Shorty rode over to inform Charley about the change in plans he started thinking about settling down in one place for a while. When he met up with Brad and Chase he had just quit riding for an outfit out in New Mexico territory. The boss man he had been working for had sold out, said he was getting too old to run it anymore and was going to live out the rest of his years just taking it easy. Shorty thought about joining a trail drive going up North, but when he met up with Brad his offer to work on a full time cattle ranch sounded just like a place a man could put some roots down at. "Yep I really think I'm going to like it here," he thought to himself. "Why I might just find me some little widow woman to settle down with. " he said, half laughing out loud.

CHAPTER 4

After leaving Chase at the saloon, Brad walked down the wooden concourse towards the sheriffs office. Reaching up he pulled down on the lip of his worn Stetson hat, adjusting it to the suns blinding glare in his eyes. Noticing only a few changes had been made since he'd left this town in the valley a little over five years ago. He spotted the new café across the street from where he was passing and that reminded his stomach that all he had eaten was the hard tack out at the ranch earlier in the morning. Glancing up the main road, he saw the white church with its tall steeple, still setting up on top of the hill and he began wondering why do people always build their churches up on a hill if there's one around? Could it be to look down on all the sinners? Maybe they want to be up closer to God. What about boot hill up there? How ironic, it's probably up there so everyone can find it Come to think on it every town he ever passed through in the foothills had their church up on a hill. In fact there was one town that called itself Church of the Hills if he remembers right. Shaking his head, he thought. I'd better get some chow soon, thinking of churches and hills, and the next thing you know I will be seeing angels.

Walking into the sheriffs office, he looked over where sheriff Warner's desk stood at one end of the room. His gaze fell on a stranger sitting there. It must be one of Warner's new deputies's, Brad thought to himself.

"Where's sheriff Warner?" Brad asked as he walked up to the fellow who was watching his approach.

Smiling, the man behind the desk started up out of his chair.

"Now can I be a helping ya lad, me names Sheriff O'Mally."

Brad stopped short and looked at this giant who was rising up before him.

Now Brad always considered himself a fair size man being well over six feet, but this O'Mally he must stand at least six foot five and weigh over three hundred pounds of solid muscle. Looking O'Mally over, he saw a full head of hair as black as coal with a wisp of a curl coming down on his forehead .The curl was barely hanging into a large set of green eyes that held a glimmer of humor. A full set of white teeth smiled under a full dark mustache. Set in his face was a smashed up nose that somehow seemed normal with his features. Brad had seen this before in men who fought often and had their nose broken more then once.

"You talk kind of funny, are you one of those forner's," Brad asked?

"Well now, I be out of Dublin." said O'Mally. "If that be a forner then I guess I must be one."

"What are you doing here as sheriff? What happened to Warner?"

Tis about two years ago that Mr. Warner went to live out his years in peace me boy and at the time with nobody a wanting the job, I thought it be grand. Tis little enough work to be had for the likes of me except fighting and a man is little nothing without pride atoll. Now is there something I can a be doing for ya lad?"

"Yea, well, do you know the Steven's spread off by Droptree Canyon?"

"Aye, I be knowing the place," answered O'Mally.

"You got any idea what happened out there and who might have burned the place down? For that matter, you know where I might find the Steven's or get word of their whereabout's.

"Not really," answered O'Mally. "That been happened just before I came here. Must be three years I reckon. What I heard was that they left the area right after the fire. That's all I be knowing, little as it tis."

Brad stood there and took in a deep breath, then let it out slowly to keep control of his feelings. Yelling and taking it out on O'Mally would not get him the answers he needed. His mouth was dry and felt as if one of Onrey's dry biscuits were stuck on the roof of it.

"Mind if I have a drink of water sheriff?"

"Not at tall. Is over in the corner it tis."

Brad walked over to the crock-pot that was covered with a wet gunnysack to help keep the water cool. Grabbing a metal cup off the nail on the wall, he dipped a cupful out. He slugged it down like a man dying of thirst. Dipping the cup in he filled it again. After finishing the second one off he was feeling a little better.

"Where can I find Warner?" Brad asked as he hung the cup back on the nail.

"What's this all to do with you Lad, our ye kin or something?" asked O'Mally

"Yeah, you can say that" answered Brad.

"Well let me be a locking up and I'll be a showing ye the way over, I kind of would like to know meself what's agoing on." said O'Mally

O'Mally turned toward the wall and picked up the shotgun that was leaning their "Come along me lad." Said O'Mally.

"I wish he would stop calling me his lad," Brad said to himself," why he can't be any older then I am." Looking over to O'Mally he thought," well on second thought, as big as he is I guess he can call me anything he wants, as long as he keeps it in a reasonable tone of voice."

Closing the door behind them, O"Mally looked over to the hitching rail and asked. "Where's your horse?"

"I left him tied up down by the saloon."

"Well I be agoing over to the livery to get mine,

shall we be a meeting there?" Asked O'Mally.

"Sure Sheriff, but I told my partner that I would meet him here. He should be along pretty soon, then well be over."

"Will take me awhile to saddle me horse for sure, so I'll be off and get to doing."

Walking back to the saloon Brad was feeling anxious, wanting to find out as soon as possible what had happened out there at the ranch. Reaching Big Dun, he pulled the slipknot that was holding him. He was just about to step up into the saddle when he saw Chase riding in.

"Did you find out anything at the sheriffs office?" Chase asked.

"No, it seems like they hired on a new sheriff since I was hear last. I was just waiting for you. Were going to ride out and see Sheriff Warner, maybe he can give us the answers were looking for."

"What's the new sheriff like Brad? Think you can trust him?"

"Chase all I can say is you have to see him for yourself. Laughing he thought, "I can't wait to see his reaction when he comes face to face with this sheriff." Brad knew Chase had seen his share of sheriffs over the years, but doubt's very much that he has ever run across one like this O'Mally fellow.

CHAPTER 5

When Brad and Chase reined up in front of the livery, O'Mally was leading out a big bald face bay. Putting his foot in the stirrup he bent his right knee and gave himself a short jump to haul up into the saddle with the least amount of pull as possible. His large bay stood square and adjusted himself for the excessive weight. Settling in he rode over next to Brad.

"O'Mally this here is my partner Chase, Chase this is Sheriff O'Mally." Chase sitting on his short-legged roan, had to look up at O'Mally when Brad introduced them to each other. He could not believe how formidable horse and rider looked together, their size was immense. The first thought that entered his mind was that he was glad that this O'Mally fellow was one of the good guys, he wouldn't like to second-guess an outcome if it came to a confrontation with him.

"Nice meeting you sheriff." Chase said as he put his hand up to his hat and tipped its brim slightly.

"Tis my pleasure to be sure." answered O'Mally," Best we be on our way lads tis a ride we have ahead of us."

Within an hour they were pulling up in front of a one-room cabin. Standing on the porch watching them approach was an old man that Brad hardly recognized, the last time Brad had seen Warner, the sheriff was already in his sixties, but things being as quite and peaceful as they were at the time, he had very little problem keeping things under control. Seeing him now, Brad doubted if the man could even make his rounds if he were still sheriff.

"Afternoon Warner, remember me? Brad from over at the Steven's spread?"

Warner looked up at Brad and said. "Light down and come on in."

Turning he walked into the cabin. Going over to the wood stove he picked up the soot- blackened coffee pot.

"Grab a few cup's off the shelf over their O'Mally, you two boys go ahead and sit"

As Brad and Chase sat down at the plain plank table watching Warner pour them a hot cup of coffee, not a word was exchanged. Finally after setting the coffeepot back on the stove, Warner walked over and took the only remaining empty chair. Looking over at Brad he said. "How ya been boy? Haven't seen you for awhile."

"Been working the trails, got a stake and went in with Chase here. We bought a nice herd down South and brought them up here to put out on the ranch. What happened Warner? Where is everyone?"

"Brad I don't really know what happened out there, the only thing I do know is that nobody has seen hide nor hair of your family since. We went over every inch of the place and never found a thing, haven't to this day."

"Didn't they tell anyone they were leaving or what happened out there?" "Well Brad that's what so strange, nobody ever saw them and the only reason we knew about the fire is that old man Thompson went over to see about buying a horse that your ma had told him about the week before when she was in town. When he got out there, that's how he found the place, just like it is today.

The place was burned to the ground and no one was around. Everybody just sort of figured after the fire that they up and left to stay with relatives somewhere."

"My folk's never had any relatives living. They lost them all during the war. It was after the war that dad brought ma out here to get away from all the bad memories. I can't believe dad would ever leave. It's not like him, he would have rebuilt, I'm sure of it."

"Brad I thought you knew." said Warner.

"Knew what?"

"About your dad. He died about a year before the fire at the ranch."

"What! How? How did he die?"

"Well Brad, it seems like he had an accident while he was out rounding up some cattle it took us all by surprise."

A shocked look passed across Brad's features and he sat there in a moment of stunned silence.

"Tell me all you know Warner about what happened and don't leave anything out, I want to know everything, and think back where you might figure ma and Kate went."

CHAPTER 6

It was nearing dusk when Brad and Chase finally rode into camp. Brad sliding down from his saddle he felt drained. He hadn't eaten all day and figured he would feel better once he got something in his gut "Hope you got some chow ready Ornery. I'm hungry enough to skin and eat one of them mules of yours."

Ornery standing next to the cook wagon, turned and looked in Brads direction, "Got the norm Brad, beans, stew and sourdough biscuits, there's still a little pie left, should be enough for you two."

Grabbing a metal plate from the wagon, they walked up to where the cook pots where hanging over the fire. While they were dishing up their grub Shorty came up and asked Brad. "Want I put your horses up?"

"Yea Shorty, were done with them for the day, but

I want to get an early start in the morning, I'll let you know later on who all will be going."

"Okay boss."

As Shorty walked off to go take care of the horses, Brad and Chase sat down and dug into their chow. They were to busy eating to do any talking. Ornery came over to the fire carrying metal coffee cups. While filling each one and handing them out, Shorty came back to the fire.

"You got anymore molasses to put in that coffee?" asked Shorty.

"I swear you and your sweet tooth are going to be the death of me yet."

"Now don't be picking on Shorty," said Chase. "I could use some of that sweet stuff myself, this here coffee could melt a horseshoe."

When Brad and Chase were done eating and all of them had settled down over their cups of coffee Ornery asked. "What happened to the place Brad?"

"I don't know Ornery, nobody seems to know anything or for that matter where anybody went." Looking over at Ornery he dreaded the news he was going to have to tell him. His dad and Ornery went back along time.

"When I met with sheriff Warner he gave me some news about dad It seems he had an accident about a year before the fire, sheriff said he got thrown while rounding up cattle out at Wind Basin Creek. Said when they found him he still had his foot caught up in the stirrup. He must of hit his head pretty hard when he was dragged by those basin rocks, killed him outright"

Staring into the fire, Ornery's shoulders slumped and he dropped his head. He felt a hard knot inside his stomach. Jim, Brads dad was the only real friend that he can ever recall having. "Your dad Jim was too good a rider to get his foot caught in a stirrup. I seen him haul off a bucking horse to many times, something ain't right here Brad."

"Well I'm just telling you what the sheriff told me Ornery."

"What did your ma and Kate do with your dad gone?"

"They couldn't run the cattle by themselves because of the distance they would have to drive them every year, sold off all of them and went into raising and selling horses. Kate being the good rider she is, that would fit right in for them. I guess they were doing pretty good until the fire."

"What happened to the stock? They must have had brood mares and colts."

"Nobody knows, they could have taken them along with them, or they could be running loose out in the canyons somewhere."

All of a sudden there was a commotion on the other side of the wagon, Curly came around dragging somebody with him. "Found this kid sneaking up on the camp over behind the cook wagon." Swinging the boy around, the light from the fire fell on the boy's face; he was in his middle teens and of Mexican decent.

"Jose, what are you doing here? Where'd you

come from?"

"Senior Brad, I come looking for you. I was not sure you are here, so I wait and see. It's not safe here now, but I must find you to give you this." Reaching into his pocket he pulled something out and held it up in his palm toward Brad.

Picking the item up in his fingers Brad turned toward the fire to see what he was holding. Looking at it he recognized the silver beret he had picked up in Mexico on his first trip there and brought back to his kid sister Kate, thinking at the time it might get her to start acting more like a girl.

"Jose, where did you get this?"

"Your sister, she give to me, tells Jose to find you and you would know it was from her."

"Brad who is this kid?" asked Chase.

"His mother was our housekeeper, he was born on the ranch about the same time as my sister Kate. His father was a Vaquero that dad hired to take charge of the horses. That's how Kate learned to ride so well. Jose and Kate practically grew up together on a horse."

"Why are you hear alone? Where's my sister and your family?"

"My mother she is with your mama and sister. When this happens at the ranch, my father and the men who worked for your family were out moving the horses to higher ground for spring pasture, I was here alone with the senoritas when they come."

"Who? Who came?"

"Don't know Senior Brad, they come and tell your

mama to get some things, then they burn the place down, then they take us away. I get free, escape, then I look for my father. When I find him, they are all hiding in Droptree canyon off from the valley floor. They have everything, he say when he comes back and finds what happen, they gather all the stock and take it there to hide in case the men come back. I hide with my father and go into town everyday to see if you have come back, we don't tell no one, we don't know whom to trust. My father he is to old to fight them."

"Jose! Where's my family?"

"When we leave here, they take us north for many days, then my mother she tell me to run, to get back and find you and my father."

"How long ago was this?"

Jose, looking down at the ground said in a low voice. "Almost three years now senior."

"So nobody knows where they are?"

"Oh no senior, we know where they go, Jose heard men talking before I run away. They take them to their ranch near Sonora."

"They want your sister to marry the big mans son."

"What? Why would he want that? She don't own the ranch or anything."

"Don't know senior, all Jose hears is she is to marry big mans son after her sixteen birthday."

Brad thought for a minute, Kate was about ten when he left. He's been gone almost six years, so that would mean she must be close to that now.

All these questions were going through Brads

head. Why take them three years ago? Why not wait until she was sixteen? Why her? Most important is how much time does he have to find her before this farce of a marriage takes place?

CHAPTER 7

"**M**a, I won't marry him, I just couldn't!" Sitting down on the bed, Kate put her head into her hands and started crying.

Connie stood there looking down at her daughter. Kate with her long thick black hair, icy blue eyes and fiery deposition was everything that Connie had left in the world since her husband Jim's death and Brad leaving home. She felt so helpless, has ever since this nightmare began almost three years ago. She thought by now that Jose would have found Brad and they would have come to rescue them, but it's been too long, it's obvious no one is coming to help them.

Connie's mind started drifting back to the day of the fire.

She was sitting on the verandah enjoying what little breeze was coming up the knoll. Looking out at the land in front of her, she was thinking how much she loved this time of year. Everywhere she looked there was evidence that spring had arrived. The grass was a deep emerald green with a full carpet of purple and white wild flowers. The large mountain oaks were budding with new life. Down below her in a rocky corner of the knoll squirrels ran frolicking through the boulders. The birds were diving down to the ground, picking up whatever treasure they can find to help build their nest. Everything seems so alive and beautiful. Connie stood up stretching her small petite frame; she raised her hands up to tighten the full bun of rich dark hair. How Jim had loved this place, it showed everywhere she looked, the work he had put in building this home for her and the children. Tears started forming in her eyes, will this pain at his loss ever cease? How she wished Brad was here, but still no answer to his where about's.

The sound of approaching horses brought her out of her reverie of Jim. Putting her hand up to protect her eyes from the glare, she noticed four riders coming up the main road toward the house. Even though she was alone she felt no reason for concern; they had strangers coming to the ranch often to buy horses.

When they pulled up to where Connie was standing, the largest one of the group came forward. "Afternoon ma'am, I was told in town that you had some fine stock for sale. Wondering if we might take a look at a few?"

Connie looking at the man, who was talking, noticed he was large, well over six feet, but heavy as well. He had red hair, under his brown Stetson hat and he was wearing an expensive western cut suit that matched his hat in color. His face was round and bloated with small squinting eyes. He had freckles on his short beefy hands.

Glancing over to the younger version of him that was sitting on his horse, she thought the young man must be his Son, the likeness was extraordinary.

The other two riders she saw, looked and dressed like your ordinary hired hands. The only thing different was the way they wore their guns and the insolent look on their faces. She had seen this kind of men before. Most of the time they hire their guns out to anyone who is willing to pay enough. She figured he may need them if he's carrying a lot of cash on him around this country, he stand's out like a big bull in a flock of sheep all dressed up to the hilt. Some folk's never learn that sometimes it's safer to blend in with the things around them then to strut about like a rooster.

Pointing across the way Connie said. "Well mister, there's some over in that corral you might consider, you go on over and see what you think, if there's one you like in particular we'll cut him out for you."

Kate came out of the house when she heard her mother talking to someone, seeing the four riders heading for the corral, she approached her mother and asked. "Are they looking to buy ma?"

"They said they were looking for some good stock and we've got the best around so there's a good chance, why don't you go on over and see if they found anything that hit there fancy and I'll go get Jose to fetch your saddle in case you need it to show any of them."

When Kate reached the corral, she saw the older red hair man looking over the large dapple-gray. "He's not for sale." Kate said as she walked up to him.

"That's a shame ma'am, he's a fine looking animal."

Reaching out his hand, he said "My names Collier ma'am, this here's my boy Frank and the other two fellows work for me."

Kate reaching out took his hand to shake, she could feel the heat from his sweaty palm. Withdrawing her hand she said. "Well we have some other fine horses over here let me show you." Turning in the direction of another horse that was standing off to the other side she started to point him out, when she felt someone grab her from behind and pin her arms to her side.

"Don't yell or say a word, the man whispered in her ear and nobody will get hurt, my men have orders to shoot your ma if you so much as sneeze, so just relax and do exactly as your told."

"What do you want?"

"I told you to be quite, one more word and your ma is a goner, now you and me are going to head on up to the house and you will do just like your told."

Connie was just stepping out the door with Jose right behind her when she saw Kate walking toward the front steps with the four men following her.

"Mr.'s Steven's we know that you and your daughter are hear alone with just your housekeeper and that boy. Now you do just as you're told and your daughter here will not get hurt. You boy, go out to the barn and hitch up that wagon and bring it on over here. Ma'am you and your housekeeper go on into the house and gather up some clothes for all of you. Anything you want to keep, you better get. Don't try anything funny or my man here will shoot this pretty daughter of yours."

"What do you want? We don't have a lot of money or—"

"Shut up! Lady you have thirty minutes starting right now to get anything you want out of that house before we set it on fire."

"What? Why would you set it on fire?"

"Ma'am your time is running, you won't need this house anymore after today. You're going to have a new home where you're going, now move."

Grabbing Marie's hand Connie said. "Come on Marie we had better do as they say we can't take a chance on them hurting Kate."

Walking into the house, Connie's mind is spinning. "Thirty minutes, what should I pack? What should I take? The safe, the money and papers in the safe, I must get the deed."

"Marie, go to your room and get whatever you can of your things together and take them outside, tell the men you need your trunks that are out in the barn, then stay and pack them outside. When your done come back inside and start getting some of Kate's things and take them out, also if they should ask about me you tell them that I am packing the trunk that was in my room, now hurry." Si senorita, I will keep them outside for you as long as I can.

CHAPTER 8

Connie ran into the den and knelt down in front of the safe, with shaking hands she turned the knob in the directions of the combination. When the door finally opened, she spread her dress and filled it with all the money and papers that were inside. Closing the door to the safe she spun the dial. Rising she held the full dress up to her chest and ran to her bedroom. Kneeling down in front of the large trunk that sat at the end of her bed, she opened it and started throwing out all the blankets and linens stored there. On the empty bottom of the trunk her hands went to the corner and found the ribbon she was looking for, pulling on it the whole bottom came up showing another compartment underneath. Thank God Jim had this trunk made when they were traveling out west to keep their valuables in Connie thought as she stood up dumping all the contents out of her dress into the hidden compartment and spreading them about. Replacing the false bottom back in place, she stood up and looked around the room. She was heading toward her dressing table where Jim's picture sat when she heard someone enter the room.

"What's taking you so long ma'am? You need my boys to help?" "Ah no, It's just that I don't know what to take, or where to begin." "Well it's like I said, just take what you need or want and no more. You *have* about ten minutes left before I send my boys in here to get that trunk of yours."

A short time later Kate, Connie, Marie and Jose were sitting in the wagon with their belongings when frank came riding up leading the large gray gelding."Might as well take this fine horse, I'll just consider him my wedding present from my future bride" he said laughing as he tied the gray to the back of the wagon. "Ma what does he mean future bride? Why are they doing this?"

With tears running down her face as she watched them set fire to their home Connie said, "I don't know dear, but let's pray that the men come back before they take us away from here."

"Oh no! Ma look, they're setting the barn on fire, my stallon is in there, I have to get him out" Jumping down out of the wagon Kate started running toward the barn when Collier rode up in front of her.

"And where do you think your going pretty lady?"

"My horse is in the barn, I have to get him out, please."

"Frank, tell the boys to get this lady's horse out of

the barn and bring him along, after all we want to show her were family now don't we."

Kate just stood there, watching the large doors of the barn as the smoke bellowed out of the roof. Shortly a man came out leading her horse that was pulling back on the rope and fighting to get loose. Kate ran over and grabbed the rope, talking and stroking the scared stallion the whole time trying to calm him down. When she had regained control of him and started walking him away from the barn, she overheard Collier saying to his son.

"Looks like she's going to grow into quite a woman son, think you can handle her?"

"Don't you worry, I'll tame her or kill her, whatever comes first."

"Not until you and her are wed you won't and don't you forget it. Until you two are married I want you to be on your best behavior and I want her to come to that wedding willing. So you better sweet talk her all you can until that day arrives."

"Sure thing, I'll have her eating out of the palm of my hand in no time, you'll see. Everything will go just as you said it will."

"They better. Mount up boys I want to get to camp before dark. Let's ride."

After hours on the trail, they finally pulled up to a camp that was sitting on the other side of a low lying hill settled in a small grove of trees, so well concealed that Connie could not see the camp fire until they were upon it.

"All right ladies you can get on down out of that

wagon. Frank have Sam tie up that boy over by the fire where we can keep an eye on him, that way if anyone should get the idea to run shoot him. So you can all have the run of the camp and make yourself at home, but remember you try anything and that boy dies."

Walking over towards the fire Connie surveyed their surroundings. Besides the four men that came to the ranch, there were three others sitting around the camp. She felt drained and dirty. She could feel the grit and grim inside her clothes. Her hair was limp and dirty, falling down and around her neck. She was feeling disorientated not knowing why all this was happening. Every bone in her body ached from the fast grueling pace they had made. The ride in the back of the wagon left her bruised and sore. Every bone in her body ached and all she craved was to lie down and sleep. There were no more tears to shed; her eyes were swollen and sore. The hurt inside her seeing them burn down the home Jim had built was more then she could stand. She felt like someone was cutting her heart out. She had only experienced pain like this once before and that was when Jim had been killed. She felt Kate next to her and put her arm around her, looking at her she could see the state of exhaustion Kate was in. Her clothes were torn from the ride and stained black from where the smoke had attached itself while she was retrieving her stud from the fire.

Looking over to where the large man who called himself Collier was setting, Connie said " I think we have a right to know why where here and for what purpose, and where are you taking us?"

Collier leaning back against a tree looked up at Connie and a smile came across his face. "Yep, I guess your right, your going to find out sooner or later anyway so it really don't matter one way or the other."

Pulling a cigar out of his jacket pocket he bit off the end and proceeded to light it. Blowing the smoke upward he looked directly at Connie and said, "Do you remember your brother-in-law Shank?"

"Yes I remember him, he was my husband's older brother. He was killed running guns and contraband during the war."

"Your right on the first half Mr.'s Steven's, but wrong on the second. Oh they blew up his ship all right, only he wasn't on it. You see he lived on to profit quite handsomely during the rest of the war, in fact he made a small fortune."

"I don't believe it, he would have gotten into contact with my husband if he were still alive."

"Well that would be true ma'am if he wanted anybody to know he was still alive. But with everyone thinking him dead, there was no warrant out for his arrest. So that left him free do anything he wanted without looking over his shoulder. Seems like he had a lot of cash stashed so it wasn't hard for him to start his enterprise's up again."

"What's this got to do with us?"

"It's got everything to do with you since Shank got sick and died two years ago. Ya see I was with Shank all those years he was making all that money and the way I look at it that money should have been left to me and my boy here. But turns out that he had a lawyer up north taking care things for him and comes to find out Shank left everything he had to your husband, being he was the only family Shank had left."

"My husband is dead Mr. Collier, he was killed last year driving cattle."

"Oh I'm quite aware of that, your husband was the first obstacle I had to eliminate."

"What do you mean eliminate?"

"Well you see ma'am in case of your husbands death all that money goes to his children and seeing that no one has seen or heard from your son Brad, that just leaves your daughter Kate. It states on the papers ma'am that in three more years on her sixteenth birthday she will be one rich little lady."

"I don't understand, why are you doing all this now when you just said she won't get any money for another three years? My husband's accident was last year, none of this makes any sense."

CHAPTER 9

Daylight was just awaking over the brim of the distant hills with a soft golden glow. Shadows still stood amongst the trees that confirmed night had dwelt among them just moments ago. Brad woke up to the sounds of the camp beginning to stir. He could hear Ornery moving about his cook wagon moving pots and other items in the course of preparing breakfast. The sounds of feet shuffling around and walking as other men were starting their day.

Laying there in his bedroll, Brad thought about all the things he had learned since yesterday morning when he had been out at the ranch. As much as he tried he still couldn't come up with any reason or for that matter anyone who would do this to his family. Sitting up he picked up his boot and shook it out, making sure no little critter had found his boot to there liking to sleep in during the night After repeating the action with his other boot he proceeded to slip them on. Standing up, Brad stretched out his stiff muscles and ran his hands through his hair. Reaching down he grabbed his gun belt, slipped it around his slim hips and secured the buckle. Pulling out his colt 45. He checked his loads and spun the action to be sure no dirt hampered any movements. Sliding his colt back into his holster he then reached down and grabbed his hat. Hitting it against his knee, most of the loose dust and grime flew off. Setting it on his head he walked over to the early morning fire. He picked up a cup and proceeded to fill it with hot black coffee.

"Morning, some hot water in that pot over there on the coals if you care to wash up." Ornery said.

Running his hand over his jaw, Brad could feel the three days growth and grime that had settled in.

"Well thanks Ornery I sure could use a shave."

After finishing his coffee Brad lifted the pot of hot water and carried it over to his gear. By the time Brad had returned to the fire sporting a clean face and fresh shirt, most of the crew was standing or sitting around drinking coffee waiting for Ornery to ring the breakfast bell.

Brad could feel something cold and wet on the palm of his hand, glancing downward he saw Pard standing next to him. Kneeling down, Brad ruffled the big dog's head. "Well *good* morning Pard, how ya doing boy?" Wagging his tail with great enthusiasm Pard let out with a short bark.

"Now don't be getting him playing around my

cooking, I get enough dust in this here gravy as it is without that dog's help." Ornery said.

Standing up Brad walked over and fetched himself a metal cup off the back of the cook wagon. Returning to the morning fire he picked up the soot blackened coffeepot and began pouring some into his cup.

CHAPTER 10

Brad looking over at Chase, could see the questions in his friends' eyes as he lifted his coffee cup and took a swallow. Letting out a slow sigh Brad said. "Can't think of any reason for all this, gesturing out towards the burnt out homestead, but I have been thinking on how to find ma and Kate." "Like what?" Asked Chase

"Well first of all we know they were taken up towards Sonora. We also know from what Jose told us that we are looking for a large red hair man with a son who looks like him, Seems to me there can't be to many around that would fit that description. Now it's a good *six* days of hard riding from here and nobody up in that area would know you or Shorty. If we leave today we could be up there before the end of the week. Once we get there we set up a base camp outside of town. Then you or Shorty can go into town and ask around about any ranches that might be hiring help. The rest of us will wait at the camp until we hear from you."

"Sounds like a good start to me." said Chase.

"Who all is going and who's going to stay and watch the herd?"

"I'll send Jose to get his father and the men working with him. Curly and the boys can wait here for them and tell them to take the herd up to Droptree Canyon with the rest of the stock. They can all wait there for us to return."

"Ornery I'll need you to pack them mules with plenty of provisions, we can't make any time with the wagon so will leave it behind. Shorty I want you to saddle Dun and Chase's horse Slide, also pick out a half dozen good ones to take with us. We may need them for ma and Kate and to switch so we can make better time. Make sure Ornery gets one reliable, he hasn't ridden much lately driving that wagon."

"I'll saddle that paddle footer for him. That horse is as smooth as a rocking chair, which is just about his speed," Shorty said laughing.

"Why you young pup, I was riding horses long before you were born, just because my bones ache now and again don't mean I'm over the hill! And another thing"—

"Rider coming in Boss" yelled Curly.

Brad, Chase and the rest of the men turned to see a giant of a man on a large stocky horse riding toward them. O'Mally rode up with a large grin on his face and he yelled out "Top of the morning to ya lads."

"Morning O'Mally." answered Brad. "Light down and have some chow. Ornery's just starting to dish it up."

Dismounting off his horse, O'Mally turned to see Shorty walking up to him. "I'll take care of him for you sheriff," Shorty said, as he reached out for the reins O'Mally held in his hands. "Why thank you lad." he said looking down at Shorty. "Ye be careful with him now." As he noticed Shorty didn't even come up to his bay's shoulder.

Brad laughed at O'Mally's remark and said. "Don't you worry none about Shorty, he'll have that horse tying the rope up for him before he's done with him."

Sitting over breakfast Brad informed O'Mally of everything Jose had told him the night before and of the plans they were making to go look for his family.

"Well now I think it's a grand idea you have and I be agoing with ya" said O'Mally

"Sheriff, you don't have any jurisdiction out of this county."

"Don't matter none. When it comes to stealing woman and ye fathers been damaged a man is not a man if he turns his back on what is right. A man is nothing without his pride me lad, remember that."

"But what about the town? Who will take care of things while your gone?"

"Me deputy can keep an eye on things for me. It's been quite it has."

"No doubt we can use your help sheriff. We have no idea what we may face when we get there."

"It's settled then. I be going to town and getting me gear. Should be back before long."

Sitting there finishing his coffee Brad watched O'Mally ride off toward town. Looking over to where Chase was setting checking and loading his colt 45. Brad felt good about the men that were going with him. He knew Chase had a past reputation with a gun. He had seen Chase use it on more then one occasion and every time the look and stance would be the same with the gun becoming an extension of his arm. Anyone could tell that he was a dangerous man to confront.

Chase looking up saw Brad watching him.

"Best to make sure everything's working right, no telling what we might run into."

Nodding Brad smiled at his best friend and said. "You know this isn't your fight Chase."

"I knew you'd think that Brad, but when we became partners your business became my business. The only thing that has me concerned is that we get there in time."

"Me to Chase, me to"

Sitting on Dun, Brad looked at the men who were mounted and ready to ride to who knew what kind of hell, to help him find his family. Chase his best friend, Ornery his dad's best friend, Shorty whose loyalty was beyond any price he could be paid, and O'Mally, a gentle forner who had never met his family, but believed in self pride and the honor of women.

Looking up to the clear blue sky full of white puffy clouds, Brad closed his eyes and took a deep breath. "Pa if you can hear me, please help us find them safe and sound".

"All right men, let's go find them," Brad shouted.

CHAPTER 11

As they were leaving the valley and climbing up into the foothills, Ornery looked behind him and saw Big Bear Valley lying miles down below them. Thinking as he rode he let his mind drift back over the years to the first time that he had ever met Jim, Brad's dad. Back to the day he thought he was going to die.

He had been trapping on the south side of Rathbone creek. The furs were the richest he had seen in years. He was in the process of lifting out a trap when he first heard the deep growl behind him. Turning slowly he looked right into the face of a huge brown grizzly. The bear was so close he could smell the bear's rank breath. He was looking right into his eyes and as his glance went down he could see a mouth full of large yellow teeth. The next thing he knew he was flying through the air. When his body slammed into the ground he could feel the pain going all the way down his side from his shoulder to his hip. Looking up through pain filled eyes he saw the bear. He was standing up on his hind legs growling so loud that it sounded like it was coming from the depths of hell. Ornery curled himself up into a ball trying to relax and look dead. As he heard the bear come closer he knew he was about to die. Beads of sweat were rolling down the back of his neck inside his shirt. Waiting for the bear to finish him off, flashbacks came of stories he had heard about bears tearing a scalp completely off, of some people being completely disemboweled from one swipe of those mighty claws. He lay there praying it would be swift. His head had popping sounds going through it and he assumed it was from the pain. His only wish that he would pass out before the end came.

Suddenly he was grabbed and flipped over. "This is it." He said to himself. He waited for that final swipe with those claws that would end his life that was only middle aged. He was only aware that he was holding his breath, when all of a sudden he heard a voice telling him it would be all right. Opening his eyes he saw a man leaning over him with something in his hand. He felt something forced into his mouth and then a burning sensation as it went down. Coughing he came out of the legacy he was in and for the first time saw a face with a smile on it and heard a voice say. "You'll live. The names Jim Steven's, if you'll just lie still there I'll go get my stock and then see if we can fix you up some." Turning he walked away toward a grove of trees. Ornery wanted to cry out not to leave him there with the bear, but found he was too weak and all he could do was groan. He must have passed out for a while. The next time he opened his eyes there was a packhorse in his line of vision. He looked anxiously around trying to see where the bear was. His eyes landed on a figure bending over some kind of bag. "Don't he know about the bear? He'll be killed." Ornery tried to rise and warn him, but could only lift his head. His whole side and arm felt like they were buried in sand. The figure stood up and came toward him. "So your finally awake." He said.

"Who are you? Where's that bear?"

"Well like I said before, my names Jim Steven's and as for that bear, I been tracking him for days, ever since he killed my stock. Got me a ranch about ten miles from here. Anyway, he was so intent on killing you, he never even seen me come up on him. Plugged him right behind the ear and he just dropped."

"Is he dead?"

"As dead as he's ever going to get. I already skinned him. Figure he'll make a nice rug for the place."

"How long I been here?"

"Long enough for me to get your wounds cleaned up and for you to sleep off a fever."

"Thanks much, I was going to meet my maker for sure if you hadn't come along. By the way my names Jack, but all my friends call me Ornery after all the years of living alone with these here mules."

"Well Ornery if you're up to it, lets say we head

on back to my ranch, I'm tired of my own cooking."

"Well hell Jim, I'm a good cook if that's all you need"

"Don't doubt you a bit Ornery and some day I may just take you up on it and see how good you are, but today is not the day."

Jarring back to the present Ornery felt tears on his cheeks for the friend who had saved his life. Ornery never left after healing up from that bear. Jim did try Ornery's cooking and found out he was a great trail cook and kept him on. Ornery stayed with him right up till the day Brad was leaving home and Jim asked him to go along and look after his boy.

Reaching inside his shirt Ornery felt the bullwhip wrapped around his waist. "I did what I could Jim." Ornery said half out loud. "I give you my pledge today though, that I will find them and make them pay for what they done to you and your family. I owe you that and then some for saving my life and being my friend."

CHAPTER 12

"Shouldn't be more then another ten miles or so from here." Ornery told Brad as they sat besides a small stream watering their horses. It had been a rough ride the last few days. Changing horses often and with just a few hours sleep each night they had made better time then Brad had anticipated. Looking over at Ornery he asked. "You've been all over this country Ornery, where do you figure a good place would be for us to lay out a camp?"

"Well now, theirs a good spot east on the other side of town. It goes right up into the pines with plenty of grass. Has a creek that runs year round so we wouldn't have any worry about water and theirs a crop of boulders on one side, with hills on the other. Can't be seen until you walk right on top of it."

"Sounds good to me. What do you think Chase?"

"As you say, he knows the country. If he says it's good, I'll take his word on it."

"Fair enough. Lets get moving. We can be there well before dark if we set a good pace."

A few hours before dark Brad crested a knoll and looking down all he could see was a cluster of boulders.

"We'll have to cut our own trail going down. It's an easy slop if you keep to the right side," Ornery said. Then taking the lead he started down.

Chase being the third in line was taken back when he saw Ornery disappear into the mass of boulders, but as he followed Brad down into them he saw where there was an opening hidden by the hill. He noticed a faint deer trail winding down in the same direction Ornery was leading them. That trail could explain how Ornery was able to find this site. Coming out on the other side he saw a small meadow right below them with a full running creek that sparkled like millions of tiny diamonds as the late afternoon sun reflected off the water.

Riding over to a grove of trees that gave off plenty of shade, Ornery started to dismount. "Don't want to get no closer to that creek, skitters can get pretty thick up here at night Come on Pard, we got our work cut out for us. Let's get to doing."

"Brad I think I'd better go back up where we cut our trail and put some brush around. We don't need anyone stumbling across us."

"Good idea Chase, I'll come along and give you a hand. The rest of you can start setting up camp while were gone."

O'Mally having led his horse over to the picket line Shorty had set up, took out a gunnysack and started to wipe down his big bay.

"These guys really got their exercise in the past few days." Shorty said.

"To be sure." answered O'Mally," I'll be giving ya a hand with the others as soon as I be done with him."

"Appreciate that sheriff."

"Now please don't be calling me that. The names O'Mally. I be no sheriff in this county."

"Sure thing." answered Shorty, as they proceeded to settle their mounts down for the night.

Sitting at the campfire later that evening. They all discussed plans for the following day.

Brad looking them all over said, "I think it would be best if Shorty went in on his own to feel things out. He can ask around like he's looking for work. Having worked on ranches down south all his life he knows all the brands in case they should ask who he's ridden for in the past. We can wait here and rest up the horses until he comes back."

"Think I should go with him?" Chase asked.

"No, I think it's best nobody see's you until we locate them, Shorty may not be as big as some men, but take it from me, he can take care of himself."

That next morning riding down toward Sonora Shorty could see it nestled down below him. Reaching up he started twisting the end of his long handle bar mustache, pondering over what he needed to do as he went. As he entered the outskirts of town he saw it was like any other small town in the foothills, one exception being it had a nice hotel, not just rooming houses. Further down and across the street was a general store and a barbershop. Past that was one of the towns many saloons. Looking at the hitching rail in front, he could see only one horse standing alone. The way he was three-legged standing with his head down and his eyes half closed it seems he had been tied there for a long time. Riding up to the rail Shorty thought to himself, well this might be as good as place as any to start.

Walking through the double swinging doors, Shorty stopped to adjust his eyes to the dimness inside. The place was the same as dozen of others that he had been in over the years. The long polished bar along one wall and wooden table and chairs set around the rest of the room. He looked the place over and saw that he was right in his thinking. There was only one other customer this morning and from the looks of him he'd been here for a while. That means the bartender shouldn't be too busy to talk.

As Shorty walked up, the bartender asked. "Morning, what will it be?"

Shorty looked at the person who was talking to him. Seeing a young tall, thin, sandy hair kid kind of took him by surprise. Just my luck thought Shorty, my first stop and I get a running nose kid who probably don't know his last name. "What you doing behind that bar kid? Ain't you a little young for this kind of work?"

"No sir, I'm eighteen this year and I need the work to help out my folks. I open in the mornings and do the cleaning up around here. It's not so bad."

"Well I'll have a cold beer if you have such a thing, and some information if I can"

"Now I can fix you up with the beer, but as for the information that depends on what you need to know."

'Well I'm looking for work and thought someone in here might know of any spreads that might be hiring."

"Hmm now let me think a minute. Now there's the Double T that's a fair size outfit, they hire extra help at times."

"Hope they don't have a son working the place. Every time I ever worked with the kid of the boss I had trouble."

"No they got no kids working out there. In fact the only place I know of that has a kid that's trouble is the Collier place. That red headed, hot headed."

"Did you say red headed?"

"Yea, why?" he asked.

"Oh, ah, well you said he was hot headed, kinda funny," Shorty said chuckling. "Red head, hot head."

"Yea, that is kind of funny," the kid said laughing.

Shorty taking a drink of beer was thinking fast. This may be the one, I need to be careful and find out without this kid getting suspicious. "This Collier place, what direction is it? I aim to go the other way."

Laughing the kid shook his head and said. "Can't blame you much with that bunch. Shouldn't be a problem though, they're south east of us near Toulume, and the Double T that I was telling you about is straight north about five miles. You can't miss it."

"By the way, what's the brand of this bunch near Toulume? Case I run into any riding for them, I can stay clear."

"Well it shouldn't be hard to spot, it looks like this." Taking his finger he drew a picture on the bar in the moisture that had settled there from Shorty's glass.

Looking it over, Shorty stored it in his mind, then picked up his glass and finished his beer. Setting the glass down and moving it over the drawing to erase any sign of it. Taking a silver dollar out of his vest pocket, Shorty laid it on the bar. "Here's for the beer and the rest is for the information, but do me a favor will you? If you see any of that bunch, don't tell them about me looking for work. I wouldn't want them to come looking to hire me."

Seeing the dollar, the kid broke out in a large grin and with a sparkle in his eye's he said. "Oh don't you worry none, I wouldn't give them the time of day if they asked me."

"Thanks! Be seeing ya kid."

Mounting up, Shorty started riding back to camp. He couldn't believe his luck at finding out about this Collier outfit on his first stop. Of course it may not be them that took Brads ma and sister, but it's a start. He couldn't wait to get back to camp and tell them the news.

CHAPTER 13

Chase spotted Shorty coming down the trail and yelled at Brad. Turning he watched as Shorty rode over to camp. As Shorty pulled up and started to light down, Chase noticed the big grin and excitement on his face.

"What did you find out Shorty?" asked Brad.

"Well you won't believe this, but at the first place I went to, this kid told me about a bunch who go by the name of Collier. The boss has red hair and a boy that looks like him. They got a place south east of town, around a place called Toulume."

"Well hell; that's just south of where we are now. Maybe eight or so miles. Let's go get-em." Ornery said.

"Hold it Ornery, I know how you feel, but we have to make sure this is the group were looking for. We cant go off blind and half cocked." said Brad.

"The way I see it, someone's going to have to check the place out and I think that someone should be me." said Chase.

"Why you Chase? Why not Shorty?"

"For one thing, this kind of rubble are more apt to hire somebody like me that can use a gun then a cowboy. I doubt ranching is the main thing going on down there."

"He may have a point," said Ornery. "Chase could go in there like a drifter or something and find out if the women are there."

"Alright, but your not to do anything except look around and then get back here to let us know what you found out." said Brad.

"I'll go get Slide for ya Chase."

"Thanks Shorty."

"Ornery can you draw out the area and show me where you think this place is at?" asked Chase.

"Sure thing." Squatting down and smoothing out the dirt, Ornery picks up a twig and starts drawing out a crude map, explaining to Chase as he goes along.

"If all goes according to plan I should be back here before dark. If not, don't worry, I'll be back as soon as I find out what we need to know."

"Just don't take any chance's with that bunch." said Brad.

"You don't need to worry none, I've been around that kind before. Be back as soon as I can." Mounting up on Slide, Chase headed out and followed the direction's Ornery had given him. It wasn't long before Chase sighted a small herd of cattle. Riding up closer he looked at the brand, it was just as Shorty had described. Sitting on Slide, he looked around trying to locate where the main house might be when he saw a small string of smoke off in the distance. "Well now Slide, I think we are on the right trail. Let's go see, shall we boy?"

Ridding up to a house made of logs with a porch across the full length, Chase approached the hitching rail. Before he could dismount, a fellow came out the front door with a Winchester across his arms.

"You can just turn that horse of yours back the way you came and head on out of here."

"Well now, I'm looking for work and—"

"We ain't hiring." The man said cutting Chase off.

At this time a large red headed man came out on the porch. Walking up next to the other man he looked down the steps at Chase and asked "What's the problem?"

"None boss, I was just telling this guy to ride on out of here."

The big man looked Chase over, then asked. "What are you doing out here?"

Chase answered. "Like I told your man here, I'm looking for work."

"Boss I already told him we ain't hiring."

"He's right, were not hiring. So you might as well get."

Chase tipped his hat and turned Slide around, all the while he scanned the area. There was the Sorrel stud in a pen off to the side. The Gray dapple Brad had described to him was in the corral alone.

Standing on the porch watching Chase ride off, the man turned toward Collier and said. "What do you think boss? Should I follow him?"

"No need to bother Hank. He's just a drifter looking for a place to hang his hat. He got the message this isn't the place for the likes of him."

Heading back to camp Chase is putting everything together that he saw at Colliers. That must be the place. There can't be to many large red headed men that have a sorrel stud with a flaxen mane and tail in a pen. Not to mention a gray dapple gelding with a right black sock. Not in this county anyway.

Chase smiled as he said. "Hell Slide, we'll be back way before dark, let's go boy."

"So what do you think Brad?" asked Chase

"From all that you told me it sounds like it has to be the place. You and I have to go back there and find out if ma and Kate are there."

"I be going with ye." said O'Mally

"Me to." said Shorty

Before Ornery could say anything, Brad said. "No, we all can't go and risk something happening to the women. We need to find out how many men he has there and somehow make contact with ma or Kate to let them know were coming after them."

"Well, if were going after dark you better study the layout of the place real good Brad. First of all, the house sits off by itself. On one side of it, there's a heavy strand of trees that we could use for cover to get close to the house. Over on the other side is the corrals and further down from them near the barn is the bunkhouse." With a small stick Chase sitting on the ground drew the whole layout for Brad.

"Chase did you see any dogs that we have to worry about?"

"No, none, didn't hear any barking when I rode up either."

"Well that's one thing in our favor anyway."

"Ornery pack us some grub we can eat on the trail, Shorty saddle Chase a fresh horse. Were leaving right away."

Chase took Brad up the same trail he had traveled earlier that day. When they were a couple of miles from the Collier's place Chase pulled up.

"It's going to be completely dark before to much longer. I think we should leave the horses tied up here and go the rest of the way on foot. That grove of trees there is the ones that go up along the house. We need to hurry if we want to get through them before nightfall."

Using the trees for cover as they went, they got about forty feet from the house. The sun had already gone down and it was pitch black. They could barely make out a faint light ahead.

"If we focus on that light there, we should be able to make it the rest of the way right up to the house." Chase said

Before long they were squatting down behind a large tree watching the lighted windows. It wasn't long before Brad tapped Chase on the arm and pointed to the upstairs. A woman's shadow was pacing back and forth in front of the window.

The gas light behind her dim.

"That's my ma in that room."

They could see the window was open and the curtains were blowing a little with the evening breeze. There was no foliage or anything near that could be used to climb on to gain entry to the upstairs.

"How are we going to talk with her? There's no way to reach that window." Brad said. "You still got that stub of a pencil you always carried while we were on the trail to keep track of the head count?" Chase asked.

"Yea." answered Brad as he put his hand inside his pocket

Taking the pencil from Brad, Chase wrote something down on a piece of paper out of his cigarette makings. Looking down on the ground he picked up a small stone.

He wrapped the paper around it and then licked it as he would a smoke. "How good are you at throwing?" asked Chase "Had lots of practice with a rope, couldn't be much harder." "Okay, the next time she walks by that window throw this into it"

Watching, Brad saw the shadow starting to walk in front of the window. Holding his breath he tossed the packet up toward the window.

"Did it go in?"

I'm not sure it's to dark. I couldn't follow it."

Eyes staring they looked at the window and watched as the shadow bent over.

"She saw it! Come on hurry." Chase said

"Why? What did you write on that note?" *"Meet*

me in the outhouse now!" Brad

"What? The first time I see my ma in six years and you set it up in the outhouse!"

"Best I could do in such short notice pal. Let's go."

Working their way around the trees they made it to the back of the house. With no moonlight, it took awhile for them to make any distance. Reaching the corner of the house Chase said. I'll wait here."

Brad continued on alone, feeling his way along the wall until he felt a section give. Knowing it to be the door he slowly opened it, just enough to slip inside.

Standing there alone in the dark with his head facing the crack of the door so as to take advantage of the fresh air seeping in. Brad began to realize how anxious he was to see his ma again after all these years.

CHAPTER 14

Connie felt something hit her arm as she walked across the room, looking down she saw what appeared to be a small white rock.. Bending over she noticed it was a wrapped piece of paper. Excited she picked it up and started opening it carefully so it wouldn't tear. After reading the note she closed her eyes and said a small prayer of thanks. Glancing over to the bed where Kate was sleeping she was glad that she wouldn't have to explain anything at this time. She had to make sure it was from Brad and not just a cruel joke. She knew it wasn't Brad's hand writing, but he could have had it delivered to her.

Leaving, she went down a short flight of stairs to the main room of the house. The big man, the one they called Collier, was sitting in a large chair behind his desk. Her eyes darted around the room and she located his son Frank. He was sitting at the table playing cards with Rick and Hank, the two men who came to the ranch with Collier the day it was burned to the ground.

Looking up at Connie, Frank sneered, "What are you doing down here?"

Connie tried to act natural; her hands were folded in her skirt so they wouldn't notice them shaking. Putting her head down in a meek way hoping they could not see the anxiety she was feeling. She answered, "I need to go outback to the privy."

Collier glancing over to Connie said. "Of course my dear, Rick can escort you out."

Rick placing his cards on the table rose and walked over to the shelf next to the door where he picked up a lamp. After lighting it he turned toward Connie and said. "After you ma'am."

Walking on the path towards the back with Rick right behind her Connie noticed how difficult it was to see, there was no moon out and it was pitch black.

She was thankful for that; there would be less chance that Brad would be seen.

Stopping a few yards before reaching the door Connie said in a medium loud voice. "Rick would you mind waiting over there away from the door? It's a little embarrassing."

"Not at all ma'am, I can watch from over there. I'll just leave the lamp here by the door, that way I can see when you come out. Wouldn't wan't you to get lost out here all by yourself now would we." he said laughing.

She waited until Rick had left. It was so dark she couldn't see where he was standing, but she knew he hadn't gone far. Opening the door she slipped inside. In the blackness of the building she couldn't make anything out. Then she heard Brad whisper "It's okay ma, I'm here" Turning she felt him next to her. With tears running down her face she slipped her arms around him. "Oh Brad, I never thought I'd see you again. We never heard from anyone all this time. You never wrote and nobody knew where you were."

"Ma! We don't have much time, is Kate here with you?" Brad asked huskily "Yes, she asleep in the upstairs bedroom. Marie is here to."

"Are you alright ma? How's Kate? Did they hurt either one of you?"

"No, were both fine. Brad your father, he had an accident"

"I know ma. We'll talk later, right now I need to know how many of them were up against"

"Hey ma'am! Are you going to stay in there all night?" yelled Rick.

"No, I'm almost ready. I'm having problems with my skirts in the dark. I'll be out in just a few minutes."

"I'll be back to get you ma. You stay on your toes and be ready for anything."

"We will Brad. There are four in the house, the one called Rick is real mean."

"You just let me worry about that. Ornery is with a few other good men and me. We'll get you out soon, you just be ready. You better go before that fellow comes in here looking for you."

Giving Brad one last hug, Connie went out the

door. She picked up the lamp and started walking toward the front of the house; she didn't have to turn around to know that Rick was right behind her.

Unmoving, Chase was standing in the shadows watching Rick and Connie returning from the back of the house. When he had heard the exchange between them and Rick laughing it took all his will power not to kill Rick right on the spot. If Kate hadn't still been in the house nothing could have stopped him. He worked his way to the door Brad had entered and said "There gone, come on lets get out of here."

Arriving back at camp Brad slid off Dun. He felt completely drained, seeing his ma, knowing she and Kate hadn't been harmed relieved the tight strain he had been under for the last week.

"Here, you look like you can use this." Ornery said, as he handed Brad a cup of coffee.

"Thanks, if I ever needed a cup of your mud it's now." Brad said, as he walked over to a fallen log and set himself down.

"What did you find out?" asked Ornery

"Their alright, met with ma for short time and she said no harms been done to them."

"So when we going after em?" asked Ornery

"First thing we need to do is get some rest, then in the morning we can sit and hash this out. We need to figure out some way to get inside that house and the way I see it I'm the only one who can."

"No, they would shoot you on site." said Shorty "You forget it's your family there after. If they knew you were still alive let alone in the area, no telling what they would do. We can't risk it."

"Well who's got a better idea?"

"Now me lad I just might."

All four of them turned and looked at O'Mally who up until then had not said a word.

The next morning O'Mally was riding up the trail heading for the Collier ranch.

CHAPTER 15

"After noon to ya sir!" O'Mally said as he rode up to the log house.

Collier standing there in the road with his legs apart looked up at this apparition in front of him. The surprising thing he noticed was the reflection of the sun on the badge pinned on O'Mally's shirt.

"What can I do for you sheriff?"

"Well now I be looking for a man who shot up one of our leading citizens. I be following him for days. Ye wouldn't happen to have seen such a fellow lately?"

"That depends sheriff on what this fellow you're asking about looks like."

O'Mally gave him Chase's description.

"Yea, we seen him, rode through here yesterday. Told him to keep on riding. If you get moving sheriff you should be able to catch up with him before long."

While Collier was talking, O'Mally caught a glimpse of a young girl hanging clothing on the clothesline at the side of the house.

"That you maybe right about, do you mind sir if I water me horse? It seems I will have a ride before me." O'Mally said as he stepped down from his horse.

"Not at all sheriff, the trough's up the road a ways by the barn."

It was at that moment Kate started around the corner to the front of the house and O'Mally let out with a yell walking towards her. "Katie me darling, 'tis a nice surprise to see you again." Picking her up he swung her around, whispering in her ear as he did so. "I come for ya lass, don't say anything."

When he stopped and set her down, Kate froze dead in her tracks looking up at this immense man who was smiling down at her. Then she glanced over at Collier standing with his hand on his gun. She knew he would kill this man with little provocation. She didn't know who this smiling giant was, but he knew her. She also knew his life depended on her actions. Her mind was racing," gather your wit's girl" she thought "Why hello sheriff, it's been a long time."

"I, me girl, we all be wondering where you be off too since the fire at your ranch. How your mother be lass?"

"Why she's fine sheriff, would you care for a cold drink before you head out? Ma would welcome any news you may have and I'm sure Mr. Collier wouldn't mind the company." Turning she could see the coldness in Colliers eyes as he smiled and said.

"Of course not, after the long ride he's had I'm sure he would enjoy a cold drink." Walking up to Kate he put his arm around her waist and said. "We'll have to let your future husband Frank join us. Why don't I have Rick go upstairs and get them."

Kate knew what he was telling her. If one mistake was made this giant stranger was as good as dead. Smiling back at him she said. "Fine, I'll go make us some lemonade."

Walking indoors Collier cried out, "Go see to the sheriffs horse Hank and make sure you water him."

"Sure thing boss, I'll put him up in the end corral for now."

When Kate entered the room with the lemonade, she saw O'Mally was sitting on one side of the room while Collier and Frank sat across from him. When Connie and Rick came in Kate said. "Oh ma look whose here. You remember the sheriff from town. He was passing through chasing some outlaw when he stopped to water his horse."

Looking first at O'Mally then at Kate, she saw the desperate look in Kate's face. "Of course I remember him, this is a pleasant surprise sheriff."

Rising, O'Mally smiled from ear to ear. "Well now, if it isn't Miss Connie looking as pretty as ever. You still be the great cook that I be a remembering? Oh for sure to have some of your home cooking lass."

Smiling back at him, Connie was thinking, "Is he here for us? Where's Brad?"

"Well now sheriff, I do still love to cook. Why I bet you're about half starved riding all over the country. How about I go in and fix you something."

Collier spoke up. "He's on the trail of that drifter who came through here yesterday, I don't think our good sheriff has time to dribble over your cooking."

"Ah, but for sure I do, never was one to miss out on good home cooking. Rare it is indeed to come across. Do worry none, I will catch up with my friend down the road, fear not. If it's all the same to you my friend."

Collier thinking serious on what O'Mally had said, thought maybe it would be a good idea to be friendly, feed him and send him on his way. Then Rick and Hank can follow him out and dispose of him down the road. Most people will think he caught up with that drifter and got shot for his trouble.

"Perhaps your both right We wouldn't want the sheriff to think were not neighborly. Kate, why don't you go and fetch Marie, then the two of you can help your mother in the kitchen."

After Kate and Connie had left, Collier said. "Care for a "real" drink sheriff?"

"Thank you no. I think the lemonade will be just fine."

"Very well, if you'll excuse me for a moment, I need to get a bottle from the other room. I won't be long."

Walking into the kitchen he looked first at Connie and then at Kate. "I don't know what you two think your doing inviting that sheriff to supper, but I will tell you both one thing, If he gets any hint what so ever that everything here is not cozy, Rick will put a bullet right through that sheriffs head, and yours to lady. Remember we only need your daughter, you're alive as long as you don't cause any trouble. Now if you want him to ride out of here the way he rode in, I don't want to see no whispering or anything else done that might give him the wrong impression. You ladies visit nice like and feed him good. If you behave and don't do anything stupid, your friend can ride on out of here with a full belly of home cooked food. Otherwise he will leave with a gut full of lead. Do you ladies understand?"

Kate thinking of the large smile and twinkling green eyes, felt a shiver go up her spine. "No," she thought, "we can't do anything that may jeopardize his life."

"Yes Collier we understand, you have no need to worry, we won't give you away."

After Collier left the room Kate turned to Connie and told her what O'Mally had said about coming for them.

"He can't mean alone, Brad and the others must be somewhere near. We have to take our time and stall supper for as long as possible to give them the time they need. Stay alert for anything unusual, and whatever you do, act natural, we can't give Collier and his men any idea that O'Mally is here for us."

Thinking, Kate knew it made sense that O'Mally must be with Brad. After Connie had told her about meeting with her brother she was going out of her mind wondering how they would get them out of there. The one part she couldn't figure out was the drifter that O'Mally said he was after that came by here yesterday. Was he with them or was the sheriff really after such a man. Would the sheriff stay and help or would he leave to pursue the man he had been following.

CHAPTER 16

Concealed in the same grove of trees that they were in the night before, Brad and Chase watched as O'Mally went into the house.

"He did it, he got inside. Too bad we only saw Collier, we still don't know who else is in there.," said Chase

"Look Chase, one of them is coming out of the house now."

Watching, they saw Hank leave and walk over to O'Mally's horse and lead him down towards the water bough.

"That must be one of the men ma said watches over them. That means there could still be three in the house. I think we better sit tight for awhile and see if anymore come or go." said Brad.

After watering O'Mally's horse, Hank started leading him past the barn to the outside corral.

Suddenly the horse's head came up and his ears went forward. He gave a soft whinny and a short blow. Hank stopped in his track's and took a quick look around. "What do you hear boy? There's no horses in that barn, there all over there in that corral." Dropping the reins, Hank pulled out his gun and started toward the barn door. Putting his back to the wall, he listened for any sounds coming from inside the barn. Slowly he turned and stepped inside the big double door. Just as he entered through it, he felt something slide over him. In an instant his arms were pinned to his side. The next thing he knew there was a rope around his neck and he was jerked off the floor.

Walking up behind him Shorty said " Mister you let loose of that gun nice and easy or this here rope will yank you another foot up, and most likely I will just leave you hanging here."

"Okay! Just don't let it get any tighter. Who are you guy's anyway, and what do you want?"

"I don't think you're in any position to be asking the question's around here." Shorty said, as he seized Hank's gun.

"Good work Shorty!" said Ornery

"Nothing to it, Never knew a horse yet that wouldn't get curious when a mule's around."

"Shorty, you work your way back to Brad and tell him I'm going to take this vermin back to camp and see what I can get out of him. You tell him to sit tight until I get back."

Reaching up, Ornery grabbed the rope and jerked it free, letting Hank fall to the ground. Bending over he picked up the loose end of the rope that was still around Hanks neck and proceeded to tie him up.

"Now fella you just start walking out that back door over there and I'm a going to follow. If you get any ideas of yelling or any other fool notions just forget it cause Pard here don't like loud voices. Understand?"

Hank looked over to where Pard was sitting; growling softly and looking like all he wanted was a piece of him. "Okay, Okay, just keep that mutt away from me."

Once outside the backdoor Ornery unhitched the mule and led him out to the area where they had hidden the horses, Ornery had Hank mount up on the mule.

After tying him on and with the mule's rope in his hand, Ornery got on his horse and headed him toward camp.

When they reached the creek, Ornery pulled up and got down off his horse. Walking up to Hank he untied him and pulled him down off the mule.

"Hey, easy old man, what do you want with me anyway?"

"I want you to tell me about what's going on. How come they took the women? What happened to the ladies husband?"

"I don't know what you're talking about The girl is here to marry Frank my boss's son Don't know about no husband."

"Take your clothes off."

"What?"

Ornery looked at him while he slowly took out a

plug of tobacco and bit off a chunk. Putting it in the cheek of his mouth he relaxed while the juices flowed

"I said take off them their clothes."

"You crazy? I don't take my clothes off for you or nobody else."

"Pard I reckon he don't listen to good. Maybe you should tell him what I mean and while you're at it, tell him you don't take much to being called a mutt."

Pard started growling and Hank glanced over to see him starting towards him, when at that second, Ornery let loose with a stream of tobacco right into Hank's eyes.

"Yow! My God you blinded me, It's burning."

"Like I said, take them clothes off."

"Alright, just keep that dog away."

Rubbing his eyes with one hand, he started unbuttoning his shirt with the other. The whole time he's undressing he could not see Ornery unwrapping his bullwhip from around his waist.

"Get me some water, I can't see."

"You don't need to see nothing! Just start talking. What happened to the ladies husband?"

"Told ya, I don't know about any husband."

The next thing Hank knew, there was a stinging blow to his bare chest that knocked his breath out. Then another blow to his stomach that knocked him down on his knees.

"Talk! Damn ya, or the next one will be lower."

"Alright! Alright, what do you wanna know?"

"Start with the husband."

"After his brother died, he was to get all of his

money. Collier figured it should go to him instead."

"Did he kill him?"

"I don't know."

Pulling his arm back and up Ornery snapped the whip again, this time he cut a bloody gash all across Hank's upper lip's.

"Aye!!!"

Falling to the ground Hank rolled over on his side, his stomach retching a foul smelling pile into the dirt.

"I'm asking you for the last time, did Collier kill him?"

Choking and spitting Hank answered in a gasping breath. "No. It was Rick, he did the old man in."

"How?"

Catching his breath he answered. "We caught up with him in some canyon, Rick pistol whipped him, then put him on his horse to make it look like an accident."

"Why?"

"With him out of the way, the money goes to the kids. The boy was gone, so that just left the girl. The way Collier figured, if his son marries her all of it will go to him."

"After they killed her. Is that what you mean?"

"Yea, after her and Frank were married she was to have an accident"

"Is that a fact. And you went along with this here little plot. Killing her pa and then burning down her home. Were you the one that was going to help her have an accident too?"

"I don't know what Collier had planned for her."

"How many men are in the house with the women?"

"Old man Collier, his son Frank, Rick and myself are the only ones."

"What other men does he have there?"

"Less then a dozen. Now I done told you everything I know, I'm hurting."

"Well now that's just to bad. Sorry to hear that, but you see, I made a promise to that girl's daddy and I intend to keep it."

"What kind of promise?"

Pulling back his arm and snapping his whip, Ornery said, "Ta take care of the vermin that killed him."

That was the last words Hank was to hear. Soon he only heard a loud roaring in his ears, and sounds of someone screaming. He felt the burning pain searing his flesh over and over again.

After awhile Ornery let the whip fall to the ground beside him..He took a few deep breaths before he turned to Pard who was sitting their looking up at him with wide open eyes. Well pard, do you reckon that fellow will feel any of them sketter's out their tonight?

Brad turned when he heard a noise behind him.

"Shorty! What are you doing here? You and Ornery were to stake out the barn."

"We did Brad and we flushed one of them out that was leading O'Mally's horse over to the corral."

"So that's where he disappeared to. Where's he at now?"

"Ornery took him back to camp so he can find out all he knows. He said for us to sit tight till he gets back here."

"Well I hope he don't take to long-god, we don't know how O'Mally's doing in there and how long he can keep stalling them,"

CHAPTER 17

"Excuse me Mr. Collier, we need Marie to bring us some more wood in for the cook stove."

"Of course Mr's Steven's. Frank, tell Hank to help these ladies get some wood."

"Hank's not back yet Pa. He went to take care of the sheriffs horse."

"Well then go out to the bunk house and get Sam or somebody. Let's get this meal done already, I'm sure the sheriff is anxious to get on his way today."

"Mr. Collier, I'm sure Marie would be able to manage enough for us, if you don't mind that is." Connie said.

"Darn her, she knows I can't very well say no without making the sheriff suspicious, besides there's little chance she would run off knowing it would put the other ladies in danger. I need Rick here to cover the sheriff, "he thought to himself." "Very well Mr.'s

Steven's if that is your wish."

Turning, Connie returned to the kitchen. "It worked, Marie do you remember what you are to do?"

"Si Senorita, I will take the little mirror you give me out of my pocket when I reach the wood pile. I will hold it up to my face like so and turn around until the sun hits it. Then I am to drop it with this package of cigarette papers. I will then gather the wood and come back here."

"Yes Marie that's perfect. Now go and watch that nobody sees you drop anything while you're out there."

After Marie had left, Kate looked at her mother. "Ma how in the world did you get that tobacco pouch and what good is it going to do?"

"I don't think the sheriff is here alone. I think Brad is out there somewhere watching the house."

"What? You think he's here now? Is that why you sent the cigarette papers, like the note he sent to us?"

"Yes, I wrote a message on them telling him about us keeping the sheriff for dinner. I only hope he sees the sunlight on the mirror to notice Marie drop it. Maybe, just maybe he will find it and get our note."

"But ma, what if he don't. and he's out there waiting for the sheriff to come back out. He could do something foolish, they'll kill him."

Tapping Brad on the shoulder Chase said, "Brad! There's someone coming out of the house."

Looking over to where Chase was pointing, Brad saw a woman walking around to the back of the house.

"It's Marie, Jose's mother." Brad said.

As the three men watched, they saw her stop at the woodpile. She took something out of her skirt pocket and held it up to her face. Patting her hair she slowly turned until the item she was holding reflected the sun.

"Just like a woman, always primping, even when their lives are in danger," said Shorty. "Look, she dropped it and she's going to pick up wood. Now why would she just leave it laying there on the ground and walk off?"

"I don't know, but I'm going to go check it out"

"No Brad, you stay here. If your caught they will kill you on sight, but a drifter is another story." said Chase.

Working his way from tree to tree, Chase came up to the back of the house. Looking around there was nobody in sight Marie was already gone and back inside. Crouching low, Chase walked silently to the spot he had seen Marie drop the mirror. Glancing down he saw it lying there and right beside it a package of cigarette papers. "Connie you are quite a woman," Chase said to himself, as he picked up the items and put them in his shirt pocket.

Heading back the way he had come, Chase had just made it to the corner of the house when he saw a shadow on the ground. Someone was coming from around the corner right towards him. Pulling out his colt, Chase flattened himself against the wall. Holding his breath he waited. Within a few moments Sam came around the corner. Chase reached out and grabbed him around the neck and put the gun to Sam's head. "Not one sound or you're a dead man," Chase said, all the while bringing his colt down on the back of Sam's head, causing him to sink to the ground. Chase took a quick look around to make sure nobody else was in the area. Spotting the clothes line, he took out his pocketknife and cut two strips from it. After tying Sam up as he would a calf, so tight he couldn't move, he put a gag in his mouth. Then he laid him next to the woodpile. Taking pieces of wood off the stack he proceeded to cover him up with chunks of wood until no sign of Sam could be seen.

"Thought you were a goner when we seen that guy heading for the John and there you were right in his path. Nothing we could do to warn ya Chase, just had to sit and watch." said Shorty.

"Lucky for me I saw his shadow. Anyway he won't be going anywhere for a while. Did Ornery come back?"

"Nope not yet. So what did you pick up out there?" asked Brad.

Reaching into his shirt pocket Chase pulled out a small mirror and a cigarette pouch. "I think you have one smart ma Brad." Chase said, as he opened the pouch. Reaching inside he pulled out the papers. Spreading them out Chase saw what he knew would be there, a message from Connie that read.

"We have managed to have the sheriff stay for dinner. It's not much but it will give you a couple of hours. There are three men in the house at this time. One went to water the sheriff's horse and will be back

shortly. Hope this helps!"

Setting the note down, Chase looked at Brad.

"Well, we know for sure there's three men inside, It's likely the old man, his son and the hired man. We don't have to worry about the other one coming back, but they are going to start wondering where he's at before long, so were going to have to make our move soon."

"From what ma said last night that hired man in there is good with a gun. I don't doubt O'Mally can take care of himself against Collier and his boy, but he's not a gunman to go up against a fellow like that one. We have to figure some way to get him out of the house."

"What about the ones in the bunkhouse? Listen! Someone's coming." said Chase. Crouching down behind the trees, Chase drew out his colt and scanned the trees for any movement. His muscles tightened up as the silence screamed out at him.

"Hold your fire, Brad said in a low voice, its Ornery."

Chase looked over at Brad and saw him petting Pard. Soon Ornery was crouched down besides them.

"Welcome back, Where's your prisoner?" asked Shorty

"He won't be stealing any more woman in this lifetime." Ornery said.

Taken back by this comment, Shorty and the others looked at Ornery. Seeing the cold look in his eyes, they could well believe what he was telling them.

"Did you find out anything Ornery?"

"Yea, your pa's death was no accident son. There were two of them that did him under. There's only one left to worry about and his name is Rick. He's one of them in the house that's tight with Collier."

"How you figure we can get that cold blooded killer out of there?" asked Shorty.

"We'll need some kind of distraction to lure him out. Ma said there was less then a dozen men in the bunkhouse, maybe we should start with them."

"No, it's to risky, the first sign of trouble they'll kill O'Mally. It looks like there's only one way to go about this." Chase said as he stood up. Pulling out his colt he started checking his shells.

"What are you thinking Chase?" asked Brad.

"Well the way I see it, you just said we can't fight them without risking O'Mally and the women, so that just leaves one other alternative and that is to join them."

"What?"

"You heard me Brad. Shorty you and Ornery go down to that woodpile and bring up that fellow I left buried under the wood. Make sure he's still asleep and doesn't see either one of you."

CHAPTER 18

"Alright! Are you all sure of what you're to do?" asked Chase

"Ya, we all got it down don't we boys?" said Brad

"Sure do boss." answered Shorty

"Reckon me and Pard can handle it alright."

"Okay, I'll see you all later, lots of luck." Bending down Chase picked up the sleeping Sam and threw him over his shoulder. Making his way around to the other side of the house he walked right up the front steps. Shifting Sam's weight across his shoulders he took his fist and beat on the door.

Kate had just come out of the kitchen door with a fresh pitcher of lemonade. Walking up to O'Mally she started filling his glass.

"My lass, you have really grown and now you're to marry this lad here?"

"Why yes," Kate answered looking over at Frank.

Kate could feel her flesh crawl just thinking about the times Frank had put his hands on her.

Frank lifted his large frame from where he was sitting and walked over to Kate. "Yes sir, this here's my little bride to be." He said as he put his large arm around Kate's waist and pulled her close. As tall as Kate was she still only came up to Franks shoulder.

O'Mally with a wide grin on his face said. "Is a lucky man you are to get such a lass." And thinking to himself, he found he really thought so. Looking at Kate with her thick black hair pulled back showed a beautiful face, but it was her eyes that really took all of his attention. There was fire in them; they were so blue they reminded him of a deep blue pool of water back in Ireland. Looking at Frank with his hand on Kate's waist, it took all his will power not to get up and smash in his face. Instead he lifted his glass and took a long slow drink, getting his emotions under control.

It was right at this moment that they heard the banging on the front door.

Jumping up Collier turned toward the noise and said "What in the Sam Hill is all that banging? Rick go see what all the ruckus is about."

Rick walked across the room and opened the door, the next thing he knew he was slammed down on the floor with a heavy weight on top of him.

Everyone in the room froze as they looked at the stranger standing in the doorway with his colt 45. Drawn and ready.

"Well fancy meeting you here sheriff I thought I

lost you back there on the trail when I doubled back. You girl, nodding toward Kate. Take the sheriffs gun out of his holster real slow like and bring it over here. Don't get any funny idea's if you don't want to see the sheriff get hurt, understand?"

"Yes, I understand." Kate said as she walked over toward O'Mally.

"What's the meaning of this?" Collier asked. "What do you want? My men are outside and you won't stand a chance of getting out of here."

"Just stay quite a minute while the lady does as she was told and nobody will get hurt."

When Kate approached O'Mally, she looked up into his eyes. He could tell she was worried. "It's okay lass, just do whatever he says, everything will be alright"

Kate smiled and nodded her head. Lifting out his gun, Kate walked over to the stranger and handed it to him.

"Very good." Chase said as he put the gun in his belt. "Now you be a good girl and go sit down next to the sheriff."

Rick was squirming on the floor, trying to push Sam off the top of him.

"Lie still before I give you a permanent reason to." Chase said

"I'll kill you for this." Rick said

"Well before you do, I want you to hold up your right hand where I can see it, and with your left hand I want you to unbuckle your gun belt. Then you can stand up."

Lifting his right hand into the air, Rick pushed Sam off. After undoing his gun belt he stood up glaring at Chase.

"By the way, your partner Hank is indisposed for awhile. So don't be thinking he's going to be coming to this party. I came to show you what inefficient men you have Mr. Collier. You said you weren't hiring, but it looks to me like you could use a good hand since some of yours seems to be tied up at the moment"

"That's what this is all about? You want a job?" asked Collier

"Got your attention didn't I, although I must admit I didn't count on the sheriff being here. Now that could cause me a problem."

"Well I'll say one thing for you, you got a hell of a lot of nerve. Maybe I can use a fellow like you."

"While you're thinking on it, I think I'll have me some of that chow I smell cooking. It's been a long while since I ate." Turning towards Kate he asked "Are there anymore women in this house?"

"Ah, yes. My ma and our housekeeper are in the kitchen."

"Fine, fine, why don't you go round them up and tell them to bring some food out here. Remember what I said about getting foolish. You wouldn't want this sheriff full of holes now would ya?"

Rising Kate left and went into the kitchen. When she saw Connie she ran into her arms crying. Oh ma there's a gunman out there that the sheriff was after and now he's got a gun on the sheriff. What if Brad shows up, that man will kill him."

"What did he say he wanted?" asked Connie

"He want's something to eat."

"What?"

"He said he was hungry and we were to bring some food out."

"Well then, I guess we better do what he wants. We really don't have much choice do we."

When Connie and Kate carried the platters of food into the room, Chase was sitting at the table with his gun laying on it "My that sure smells good ladies." Chase said as he reached into his shirt pocket and pulled out his makings. "You ladies don't mind if I smoke do you?" he asked as he poured the tobacco out into the paper and started to roll it. Smiling at Connie he said. "You know ma'am I used to write notes to my gal on papers like these and throw them in to her bedroom window. It seems her pa had a dislike for me for some reason. Now I wonder why that might be?"

Connie stared at him as what he had just said went through her mind. He's with Brad; he must be the one who wrote the note the other night from him. Pulling herself together she set the platter down on the table and said. "I sure wouldn't know sir. Could it be he saw you for what you really are?"

Frank started laughing and said, "Sounds like she's got you pegged friend."

Chase laughed with him and said. "Seems your right, she surely does."

Turning, Connie went back into the kitchen with

Kate following right behind her. After they went through the door Connie grabbed Kate and pulled her over next to Marie. "That man out there, he's the one who wrote the note telling me to meet Brad."

"But ma, why would he take the sheriffs gun? If he's with Brad the sheriff would help them."

"I don't know all that's going on, but they must have their reasons. Now you make sure you don't give him away and make sure you do what ever you're told to do. Now get the bread and butter and take it on out, Marie and I will bring the dishes."

Collier walked over to the table and sat down. "You are one cold fellow." he said to Chase. "What's your name?"

Chase looking straight at him answered "Monty. Monty Sipes."

"What? Your Monty Sipes the gunfighter?" asked Rick. "No you can't be, I heard he was killed down near Mexico some years back."

"Don't believe everything you hear Rick, I know for a fact he wasn't killed cause I'm sitting right here. As a matter of fact, I was the one who started that rumor. Thought it was time to make a change. Was doing real good to, until I ran into this fellow who knew me in this sheriffs' back water town. That's why I killed him."

"Well now this does change a few things." Collier said "What makes you think I need you? I'm just a small rancher here living a quite life. I keep Rick and Hank around to keep out any trespasser's is all."

"You know that's what I thought the first time I

came by looking for work. That's why I thought it would be a good place to lay low for awhile until this sheriff got tired of running all over the country looking for me."

"So what changed your mind?" asked Collier

"Seems when I came back here, I ran into Hank out by the barn. Now he wasn't to friendly at first, but after awhile we got to talking real cozy like. He was real anxious to tell me everything he knew."

"That's a lie." Rick said. "Hank wouldn't have told you nothing."

"Is that a fact. Well Rick, he told me how you and him met up with that girl's pa out in that canyon. Now the ladies are coming in with all that good food. I don't like to talk business on an empty stomach. In fact why don't you all come sit down and join me, that way I don't have to watch my back. You to sheriff, after all you're entitled to a last meal," he said as he smiled and winked at Connie.

CHAPTER 19

"Shorty! You got your rope ready?"
"Sure Thing Brad."
"How about you Ornery? You ready?"
"Ready as I'll ever be."

"Okay, remember the only way were going to get all of them is by surprise, there's seven of them and only three of us, which don't make the odds to good."

"Four!"

"What?"

"I said there's four of us."

"What do you mean four of us Ornery?"

"You're forgetting Pard."

"Yea, Ornery your right, Pard does help bring the odds closer. I'm going up on the roof now. You two stay put until I get back and stay out of sight." Brad said.

Working his way to the back corner of the building, Brad was thinking how lucky they were that the bunkhouse was a good distance from the house. With any luck they won't even know what's going on if Chase is able to keep them busy.

Climbing up on the rain barrel, Brad reached up and grabbed hold of the porch. Pulling himself up he laid his upper half on the roof, turning he pulled one leg up at a time until he was laying flat. He kept still for a few minutes to listen for any noise from inside. Crawling slowly, he came to the stovepipe in the corner. Taking the wet gunnysack out of his shirt, he stuffed it into the pipe.

"Sorry to spoil your supper cooking fellows." Brad said to himself as he quietly went back the way he had come.

Brad had just arrived at the front door and put his back against the wall when he heard the first commotion inside. The front door flew open and in the mist of smoke billowing out, Potter the cook came stumbling out coughing and heading down the path away from the house.

"Get him Pard." Ornery said in a low voice.

Pard turned and in a few strides had reached his prey. Sailing through the air, Pard came down upon him, knocking potter full force on the hard ground as he landed. Ornery didn't watch anymore, he knew Pard would take care of that one. Turning, he saw two more coming out the door. Shorty already had his rope in the air landing around the one in the lead. Jerking the rope tight it pulled the fellow right off his feet and towards him. Backing up to the horse at the hitching rail Shorty tied his end of the rope to the saddle. Pulling on the slipknot that held the horse tied to the rail; Shorty took off his hat and swatted the horse's rear. Spooked by the sudden hit, the horse took off running, dragging his burden behind him.

Brad, seeing Shorty throw his rope over the first one, stepped out in front of the second one coming out the door. Bringing up his knee, he caught him in the groin. As the man doubled over with a yelling groan, Brad brought up his right and caught him square on the jaw, dropping him without taking another step. Grabbing him under the arms, Brad dragged him to the end of the porch. By the time Brad looked up at the door, the other three were coming out through the smoke, doubled over and coughing.

Like hitting a solid wall, the first one stopped dead in his tracks as a sharp pain pierced down the front of him. The other two behind him stumbled and fell against him. Coughing with their eyes full of smoke, they couldn't see what was blocking their path that tripped them. The one on top felt himself being lifted up in the air and suddenly there was a hard blow to his stomach, then one to his head. The pain was so bad he thought he would pass out. He felt himself being slammed against a wall and another blow, then nothing as blackness came over him.

Brad seeing the man was out lifted him and carried him to the end of the porch, laying him down besides the other one that he had dragged there earlier. Looking over to the far end of the porch he saw Shorty fighting with a fellow that stood two heads taller then him. Every time the guy took a swing at him, Shorty would duck and the guy's punch would hit air, but Shorty's two short jabs in the gut hit every time. Then Shorty turned and moved right under the next swing that was coming towards him and lifting his right leg he brought it down so that his large rowel spur came in direct contact with the shin, knocking the fellow down flat on his stomach. Shorty reached down and grabbed his head, smacking it down with as much force as he could muster. It was only a matter of seconds that Shorty had him tied and trussed up. Seeing Shorty had everything under control, Brad glanced over to the first one that came out the door. There was blood running down his shirt where Ornery's whip had pierced through it on its trail of devastation. He could see the man had no intention to move while Ornery was standing there with whip in hand.

"Where's the other one?" Brad was thinking to himself

Frantically he looked around; did he get up to the house and alert the others? Did he come out of the building? "Ornery! Did you see the other one?"

"Nobody else came out Brad, just this bunch."

Drawing out his colt 45. Brad stood on one side of the door. Peering in, he couldn't see anything through the smoke. "Shorty, you and Ornery make sure these guy's are all taken care of, I'm going up to the house."

"Don't think that's a good idea Brad.," said Ornery.

"Look, ma said they were cooking supper. That

mean's the woman will be in the kitchen. I can work my way around back and see if I can get in through there. I've got to warn Chase that one of them got away. If they get Chase we'll never get them out. They may kill all of them. Now, do as I say, and take care of things here! When you're done, I want you to round up all of their horses, just in case any of them gets a notion to ride out of here."

CHAPTER 20

"The more I think on it Monty," Collier said to Chase. "I like the idea of you coming in with us. Give Rick back his gun."

"Not just yet Collier. I'm not done eating and I don't want to spoil this good supper watching him."

"Rick won't be no trouble now that you're working for me."

"We don't need him boss.," said Rick.

"Maybe, maybe not, but he's the one that's got the gun, not you."

"Alright don't anyone make a move or this here lady will be the first one hurt!"

Everyone in the room turned towards the kitchen door where the voice had come from. Standing just inside the room was one of Colliers men. He had his left arm around Connie's neck and in his right hand he held a gun pointed at her waist.

"A group of men took out the boy's in the

bunkhouse boss. Figure they must be with this fellow here."

Looking over at Chase, Collier said. "Take his gun Rick."

Walking over to Chase, Rick picked up the gun that was lying on the table next to him. "Hand over the other one nice and slow like." Rick said while he held out his hand.

Looking over at Connie, Chase knew he had no choice but to do what Rick said. He couldn't take any chances with Connie's life at stake.

"Sure thing Rick." he said as he lifted out the gun he had in his belt and handed it over to him.

After putting the gun in his holster, Rick backhanded chase across the mouth. "I told you I would take care of you."

"Rick! That can wait, right now I need some answers." Collier said.

"Where's your men at Monty?"

"There not my men. I'm alone. "Chase said as his eyes stayed on Rick with a hard cold stare, Rick felt a small shiver of fear go through him and shook it off.

"He be telling the truth." O'Mally said. "The men our my posse that was following behind me."

"Well now is that a fact. Then you had better be calling them in here now. Tell them to put down there gun's and don't cause no problem or that little lady is going to be in big trouble. Understand?" asked Collier

"Collier, give me back my gun. You can use all the help you can get right about now." Chase said.

"How do I know I can trust you?"

"Well for one thing, that sheriff and posse were after me, not you, and the other reason is you need me to clean up this little mess you have on your hands. What do you plan on doing with the sheriff and his posse? You sure don't want to dirty your hands at this stage of your plans. Hire me on and I'll take care of them for you."

"And how do you figure on doing that?" asked Rick.

"Well the whole town knows that the sheriff here was on my trail. If they should get bushwhacked while trailing me, I'm the one that gets the blame. For that matter nobody will even know they stopped here. So you see Collier we both win.

You can go on with your little charade as if nothing has happened and I'm rid of this here sheriff and his posse,"

"If it was anybody besides you Monty they wouldn't stand a chance, but knowing your reputation I can see where you could get by with it. Give him back his gun Rick."

"Boss I still don't trust him"

"Why because he's faster then you? Or smarter? You heard what he said and he makes a lot of sense. Now do as your told."

Brad had worked his way around to the back of the house and he just caught a glimpse of a man going through the back door. "Shit, I'm to late, he's already going into the house." Brad thought. Working his way cautiously, he managed to get to the kitchen window, slowly he rose up and looked into the house. He saw the man seize Connie and drag her out the door into the other room. Looking around he saw Marie was the only one left in the room. In a few short strides he was inside the door. When Marie turned around she almost let out with a shriek seeing Brad standing there. He had his finger up to his lips, warning her not to make a sound Walking over to the door he put his back against the wall and stood their listening.

Sitting at the table, Chase stared hard at Connie, feeling his eyes on her she glanced over at him. Chase looked at the table and then pointed at the bowl of hot stew sitting there. Connie nodded slightly that she understood. For her sake he hoped she did. Chase stood up and walked over to Rick and held out his hand. With a snarl on his mouth Rick handed Chase back his gun.

"Mr. Collier, I don't mind taking out this here sheriff for you, but tell your man to let the lady go. I don't want no part of hurting any women. Killing a man is one thing, but killing or hurting a woman in this country is a sure way to get yourself hung. They'll track you down to the ends of the earth and back. It's the one thing above horse stealing that nobody will abide."

"I have no intention of hurting her Monty, you see she's my security that her daughter will do as she's told. Dirk, let her loose, I think the sheriff knows his position that we will do what ever need's to be done if he don't cooperate."

After Dirk let Connie go she walked over to the

table and started stacking the dirty dishes, Kate rose from where she was sitting and walked over to give Connie a hand.

"Now sheriff where were we? Oh yea, are you going to call your men in nice like or do we have to do this the hard way, starting with you? Asked Collier.

O'Mally looked at Collier and knew he was in a spot. He had no gun and if he called Shorty and the rest in, they would be as helpless as him. If there was only some way. He looked over at Chase and saw him nod his head towards the front door as he drew his gun and pointed it right at him.

Collier smiled thinking to himself, "This is going to work out just fine with Monty taking care of this problem, everything will be just fine."

O'Mally got up off the sofa and let out a resigned sigh. Walking towards the front door Chase came right up behind him, keeping his eyes on Rick the whole time.

Connie picked up the bowl of stew that was left on the table and started carrying it into the kitchen. Just as she was to pass by Dirk she threw the contents of the bowl into his face. Dirk let out with a bellow and all eyes turned towards him except Chase's. He turned his gun in the direction of Rick and let go with two quick shots before Rick's hand cleared leather. Chase could see the surprised look on Rick's face as he watched his gun slip out of his useless numb fingers as his leg's slowly bent at the knees. Looking over at Chase, Rick said. "I never really believed you were

Monty, thought for sure he was dead. Guess I was wrong." At least I'm going out knowing I came up against the best." Then he fell face down into a heap on the floor.

Turning, Chase glanced quickly around the room and spotted Frank, who was still sitting at the table, jump up and grab Kate around the neck with his large thick arm. As tall as Kate was she was no match for Frank's large bulk and strength.

"Hold it right now or I will snap her neck like a chicken"

Turning around, Chase had his colt on Frank.

"I wouldn't do that Monty, She'll be dead I swear it"

Chase swung his colt around so that it faced Collier. "Looks like were at a standstill Frank. You so much as mess her hair and I'll shoot him."

"No you won't, because you know I'll kill her. "Pa were going out that door and get to the horses. None of you better follow or try to stop us, or you won't see this little gal alive again."

Brad standing by back the door listening, thought, "You just come on through here you son of a bitch, and I will kill you with my bare hands."

But Frank headed towards the front door, dragging Kate with him. Collier turned and started to follow Frank, watching as Chase lowered his colt.

O'Mally standing there said." I'll ask ye to leave thee lass alone."

"You just stay out of my way sheriff and no harm will come to her." Frank answered.

Brad, seeing Frank drag Kate out the front door, turned and ran out the back. As he started around the corner he ran into Collier who was running to the back of the house when he saw O'Mally jump Frank.

Seeing Brad, Collier swung a hard right to the chin and then a short left knocking Brad down into the woodpile. Collier reached down and picked up a stick of wood and started to swing it like a club at Brad. Rolling over, the wood came down hard, right where Brad's head was a moment before. Jumping up as quickly as a cat, Brad cut in with an upper left to the eye and a downward punch to the left jaw knocking Collier over against the door. Brad then rushed in with his head down and Collier went flying backwards through the door landing near the cook stove. As Brad came into him, Collier grabbed the coffeepot off the stove and threw it at Brad. Seeing it coming, Brad ducked to the side, the pot just missing him and hitting the wall. Brad swung with his right and then with his left knocking Collier down. As Collier started to rise with blood running down the side of his face Brad said, This ones for you Pa." Then swinging his leg up he kicked Collier full in the face with his boot knocking him into the stove. Gulping deep breaths of air, Brad stood over Collier shaking, trying to get control of his emotions when Ornery came in.

"Looks like you boys had all the fun in here while we baby-sat them horses."

When Frank reached the front door he opened it and yelled outside. "Don't any of you move out there or I kill the girl." Then he proceeded out and onto the porch.

O'Mally stood there watching Frank drag Kate out the door, the whole time thinking. "He's a dead man he is."

Reaching the stairs, Frank started down them when he heard a deep growl behind him. Turning he looked right into Pard's' snarling jaws. "Call that dog off or I swear..."

While Frank's attention was deviated, Kate bit down as hard as she could on his wrist Yelling; he let her loose and with his right hand he slapped her hard across the face, knocking her down the stairs.

O'Mally seeing Kate fall growled out "He's mine, leave him be." Rushing out he jumped on Frank in mid air at the top of the stairs. Both of them fell to the bottom of the steps rolling across the ground. Frank broke free and started to get up on his feet. O'Mally swinging his leg around, kicked Frank in the face knocking him over backward. Before Frank could move, O'Mally was up and grabbing him by the front of his shirt. Yanking him up on his feet, O'Mally let loose with a swing to Frank's face. You could hear the bones break in his nose, and as the blood went flying. Frank shook his head and started for O'Mally with his head down. Just as he reached him, O'Mally sidestepped and brought both hands that were locked together down on the back of Frank's neck. Falling to the ground, Frank felt a large rock next to his hand. Picking it up he threw it at O'Mally. It glanced the side of his head stunning him momentarily, just long enough for Frank to get up and grab him around the mid section, pinioning his arms. With a strangled groan and gasping for air, O'Mally brought up his knee and hit Frank in the groin. Stumbling with blood still flowing from his nose, Frank tried to ward off the next blow and fell. Shakily he tried to rise, but fell plum back to the ground.

"Stay down ye liveried ass if you want to live. Twill make no mind to me how ye die for putting ye hands on me woman."

Turning Brad asked." Did anyone take care of the one who had a hold of ma?"

"Oh he was took care of alright, seems after your ma threw that stuff out of that bowl at him, she just went ahead and let him have it with the bowl itself. He went down nice and quiet like. Yep your ma is quite a gal."

Shaking his head Brad said. "She sure is, that she is. Come on Ornery let's get this poor excuse of a man outside with the rest of the trash."

CHAPTER 21

Dragging Collier between them, Brad and Ornery came around from the back of the house. The first thing Brad saw was Frank sitting on the ground. His face *was* full of blood and Brad could tell that Frank wasn't going anywhere for the time being. He saw O'Mally was picking Kate up off the ground where she had fallen when Frank had slapped her.

"Are ye hurt lass?" O'Mally asked as he held her up and looked at the dark purple bruise swelling up along the side of her eye.

Looking up into O'Mally's green eyes she could see the concern on his features. "No, I'm just a little shaken. I'll be okay if you wouldn't mind just holding me for a few minutes until I can stand. I think my ankle is twisted from the fall down the stairs."

"For sure lass, I be happy to hold ye."

Kate noticed his strong arm's felt good around her

and she put her head on his chest. She felt safe and secure for the first time in years. How odd that she didn't feel the repulsion she had felt so many times when Frank had touched her.

O'Mally holding Kate in his arms felt a lump in his throat and realized how natural she fit next to him

"She's going to be mine someday for sure." he thought, "No matter how long it takes to win her, she is a woman worth a man's soul."

"What happened out here? Did you get all of them?" asked Brad.

"Yep, they sure did," Ornery said "O'Mally licked that Frank real good, kinda think it rubbed him just a little much when he seen that Frank fellow hit Kate."

"He hit her! Is she okay?" Turning he started towards Kate. Ornery reached out and grabbed Brad's arm and said. "I think she's just fine now that O'Mally's holding her."

"What do you mean holding her."

"Well you know like a man hold's a woman at times."

"Why she's just a kid, I'll knock his big Irish head off."

"Now I don't think I'd be a doing that. You got to remember you've been gone for a spell, and that little gal has done some growing up some since you last saw her. I don't think she would like it much if you came butting in right about now."

"Ornery, she's been through so much."

"That be a fact Brad, but I don't think you need to

worry none where O'Mally's concerned, he seems to be a gentle enough type. Best maybe we just let them be for a time."

"Could be your right Ornery, I keep forgetting Kate's near a grown woman and has been doing pretty good up till now without me around."

Chase walked over to where Connie was standing next to Dirk's sprawled out form. Her shaking hands still holding the make shift weapon she had used.

"For such a little thing, you sure do throw a mean bowl," Chase said with a chuckle.

Turning, Connie looked at Chase and smiled.

"If it wasn't for you, I wouldn't have thought of it"

Taking a closer look at Chase, she found she liked what she saw, a man not much older then herself who carried himself with great confidence and strength.

"Are you Brad's friend?"

"His friend and his partner."

"How did you two meet?"

"That my dear is another story for another time. Right now let's say we drag this mess outside and join the rest of your family."

Grabbing Dirk by the back of his collar, Chase dragged him out to the front porch.

"Here's the other one." Chase said

Walking up to Chase and Connie, Brad said "Are you all right ma?"

"Yes, I'm fine. Where's Kate? Is she hurt?" Connie asked, as she looked around for Kate.

Looking over at O'Mally all she could see was O'Mally standing there with his back to her. There was no sign of Kate who was well-concealed in O'Mally's arms.

"Ma you go and get Kate she's over there with O'Mally. Me and the rest of the boys have some unfinished business to take care of."

Turning to Chase he said." There's three more trussed up at the bunkhouse. Bring that one along, and well get Collier and Frank. Let's haul them all up to that grove up there on the hill.

"You're the law O'Mally, what do you say?" asked Brad.

"I be no law here lad. Besides it's for a fact we hang horse thieves on the spot. Tis worse when it's a woman and for what they did. For sure they would have killed your ma and the lass when they no longer needed them. I vote the same as the rest of ye."

"That settles it then. Shorty did you round up enough horses and did you bring the gray like I said?" Brad asked

"Sure did Brad. They're their under that grove of trees."

"Are you sure you want to go through with this Brad?" "We could take them back to town with us." Chase said.

"No Chase, it has to be this way. You don't understand."

"I understand killing and sometimes a man's not the same afterwards."

"You don't need to worry none on that Chase. This has to do with family and it needs to be done to finish the whole business."

"If that s how you feel Brad, I'm with you all the way. Let's get it over with."

Come on boys, no sense in putting it off, the sooner we get it done the better." Dirk screamed and started kicking as Shorty and Ornery carried him over to the horses.

"Monty! You just can't hang us. Monty, shoot me, don't let them do it. I don't want to shit my pants!"

"You picked the brand to ride with Dirk. You knew what these fellows did to the lady's husband and that there girl's pa. You went right along with the whole thing. Put him and the rest of them on the horses and hang them. Let this be a lesson to anyone else that may think they can get away with taking a woman from her home in this country."

CHAPTER 22

L oading the last trunk into the back of the wagon, Ornery picked up the rope and started tying it down with all the others. His face was expressionless as he proceeded with his task. Shortly he was aware of footsteps coming up behind him, turning he saw Marie standing there with a small valise in her hand. "Ma'am would you like for me to put that in the back with the rest of them their trunks?"

"No senior, I will keep this with me, it is light" "Alright ma'am, come on and I'll give yea a hand up into the seat" Walking to the front of the wagon Marie stopped and turned slightly. Sensing her movement had ceased, Ornery paused and followed her gaze. Off in the distance among a large grove of trees there were five bodies swinging from separate branches.

"Come-on ma'am you don't need to be seeing anymore of this." Ornery said, as he gripped her elbow and led her to the front of the wagon. After he helped her up into the seat Ornery turned and looked back to the grove. He could make out the small group of riders sitting on their horses facing a man standing up on a large gray horse. Motionless he watched.

Sitting on Dun, Brad looked up at the man standing on the horse. He could see the sweat trickling down his forehead over his cheek, and then disappear beneath the rope that was tied thick around his neck.

"Why Collier? Why my pa? Why take Kate and my ma for three years?"

Collier looking down at Brad said. "We needed you and your pa out of the way so Kate would get the money. Figure if we did it early enough, after a few years most folks would forget all about the family. They would think they went to live with their kin somewhere. So when the time came for Frank and her to get married nobody would even be thinking about them."

"You should have known better Collier. The worst thing there is in this country next to a horse thief is a man who hurts a woman. It's a hanging offense. There's not a man around here who wouldn't string you up themselves if they got their hands on you."

With a light motion of his knees he gave Dun the signal to move, as he did so he turned and looked at Connie who was sitting on her horse not showing any emotion. In a soft voice he said. "Come on ma, let's go home."

"Brad!!" Collier yelled "Is this your way of getting

revenge? To leave me standing here till my legs give out and I hang myself? I already watched you hang my boy. So what is it? You don't have the guts to do it yourself?"

Stopping big Dun, Brad turned and faced Collier.

"No, that's where you're wrong Collier. It's not my revenge at all. You see, that big gray your standing on that Frank took from the ranch was my pa's horse. Now being the cowman that he was there were times when he would be away some distance from that horse and instead of him having to walk all over the country, he just taught him to come whenever he whistled. Good-by Collier."

Turning Brad rode up to the wagon, looking at Ornery he nodded his head.

Ornery putting two fingers in his mouth let loose with a long shrill whistle. In a few moments the large gray came loping up to Ornery empty of its burden.

"Thanks Brad for letting me be the one to call him."

"It's okay Ornery, I know how much pa meant to you and the pledge you made."

Glancing over to the grove he could see the large frame still swinging side to side from the tree.

"The main thing is that Pa got his revenge for himself and his family, which is almighty rare in these times. Just goes to show, justice comes for them that wait.

CHAPTER 23

Sitting very still on her horse, Connie looked up at the body swinging from side to side. She felt tired and numb as the memories of the last few years flashed through her mind. Tears started burning her eyes as she thought of her future without Jim and the pain was almost unbearable. Her mind went to the years of youth Kate had lost while locked away in this nightmare. The tears started flowing faster until she was sobbing out of control. She was shaking so hard she didn't feel the brush against her neck as chase's arm encircled her. Chase lifted her slowly and sat her on the saddle in front of him, Slide shifting his weight to stand with the extra burden put upon him.

Still sobbing, Connie turned and buried her head into chase's shoulder. She felt safe for the first time in so long. Chase sat as still as possible, holding this small gentlewoman, all the while looking up at the man who was hanging before him. His eyes cold and hard, he thought, dam you to hell Collier for doing this to her. May your soul rot in hell.

Hearing the sound of a horse approaching, Chase turned to see Kate riding towards them. He could see she also had tears in her eyes. Following behind her was O'Mally. Chase nodded to him and then tilted his head towards Connie's horse. O'Mally raised his arm and made a gesture that he understood. Riding over to Connie's horse he reached down and took hold of the reins then turned toward Kate.

"Come lass, let's be going from this place." he said, as he turned and started toward the waiting wagon with Connie's horse in tow.

Kate sat there watching her mother cry in the arms of this stranger who had risked his life to save them. She wasn't sure what she should do. Her emotions were mixed. This was the first time she had seen anyone hold her ma besides her pa. But she felt deep inside that for the first time in years her ma was truly safe. Kate looked once more at the grove of trees. She took a deep breath and with the back of her hand wiped the tears away from her eyes. Her emotions were still running wild, but the main thought kept running through her mind. I am free; the nightmare is really over. Her eyes flashing with new life in them, Kate thought. I make this vow, that no man will ever make me his prisoner again. I will fight to my last breath if I have to. I couldn't take any chances then that they would hurt ma, but she is safe now. God help any man who try's to do anything to her family or her again. Taking one last glance at Chase and her ma, Kate turned and followed O'Mally.

Chase sat as still as possible while Connie sobbed. Holding her he felt how small and fragile she was, and his heart went out for the pain she had gone through. He had seen his share of death and grief over the years, but for some reason nothing compared to the emotions flowing through him as he held her. His mind flashed back and for a moment he saw another face from another time. It was a woman's face framed with golden hair and deep green eyes. "No!" His mind shouted. This time it is different, she's alive, and I will see that nothing happens to her. Connie moved and Chase snapped back. He untied his kerchief with his left hand while his right arm still held her in place. He handed it to her, and watched as she wiped her eyes and tried to get control of herself.

Connie gasped for breath as the tears subsided. She looked up and saw that Chase was smiling at her. All of a sudden, she felt embarrassed sitting and bawling like a baby in his arms. She sat up straighter and tried to get her composure together. Looking up at him she said, "I'm sorry, I don't know what came over me."

Chase took hold of her chin and looked down into her eyes. "You don't need to apologize to me or anyone else. It's scum like them that causes honest folks the pain and tears. What do you say we go join the rest of your family and leave this behind." Smiling back at him with a small smile, Connie nodded. Standing with Dun at the water trough, Brad watched as Chase rode up to him with his ma. Reaching up, he lifted her down to the ground. "Are you okay ma?"

"Yes, I'm fine now, and I have never been so glad to see anyone in my life" she said laughing as she went into his arms and hugged him.

After a few moments, Brad looked at his ma and then up at Chase. Sitting there rolling a smoke, a funny smile crossed Chase's face and he said, "Well we got what we came for, where do we go from here?"

Kate looked at them and said, "I don't know what you boy's have planned, but I'm going to the first town I can find and do some shopping. How about you ma?"

"Sounds like a right fine idea to me Kate. It's been to long since we have had anything new. Let's go."

Brad and Chase stood there watching the two-woman mount there horses and start riding down the road.

Looking at Chase, Brad said, "Who can figure woman out, there going shopping after all this."

Laughing Chase said, "Yea, ain't it great to have them back. Almost forgot how much fun women are."

Brad turning to the rest of the men said, "Well, what are you all doing standing there? You heard the ladies, let's go to town, and if were lucky enough maybe we will be able to head back home by the end of the week."

Printed in the United States
64187LVS00003B/232-270

9 781598 006476